ONCE THERE WAS A WAY BACK HOME

A HOMEWARD JOURNEY
Book One

ONCE THERE WAS A WAY BACK HOME

Louise M. Gouge

CROSSWAY BOOKS • WHEATON, ILLINOIS
A DIVISION OF GOOD NEWS PUBLISHERS

Once There Was a Way Back Home

Copyright © 1994 by Louise M. Gouge

Published by Crossway Books
    a division of Good News Publishers
    1300 Crescent Street
    Wheaton, Illinois 60187

Cover design/illustration: Britt Taylor Collins

First printing, 1994

Printed in the United States of America

ISBN 0-89107-804-5

To Pat Bickers *who sent me to my typewriter with the exhortation to "Write that story!"*

To my husband, David, and my children, Jane, Christopher, Timothy, and Sarah, *who came home every day and said, "What did you write today?"*

To Dr. Leonard Wilkerson and Dr. Bob Roberts *who lent me their medical expertise and didn't send a bill!*

To Bernie Barbour *(formerly of the New England Patriots) and Derrick Williams who advised me on football.*

To Mary Busha *who took my novel to Crossway Books.*

And to all my friends *who read the manuscript and found my mixed metaphors, dangling modifiers, and typos.*

THANKS!!!

ONE

Janice Griffin reached out to shut off the irritating ring of the alarm clock, then rolled out of bed and quickly dressed for work. Unplugging the clock, she reset the alarm by the dim bathroom night-light and tiptoed to Billy's room. There she groped in the dark for the extension cord and plugged in the clock, then set it on his dresser. She resisted the urge to kiss her son good-bye. It would not do to wake him at 5 A.M.

Outside her small trailer, she paused and took a deep breath, filling her lungs with the pure, refreshing autumn air of Colorado. Then she walked briskly up the gravel driveway to the road that led out of the trailer court. Fifty yards ahead at Trucker's Haven, the usual fleet of trucks warmed up for the day's travel.

Janice gazed across the highway at the eastern horizon where the faint glow of dawn blended into the starlit sky. One more deep breath, one more moment of pleasant solitude, and then she would make her daily leap into the chaos of the diner. Eight or ten truck drivers were already there drinking coffee.

"Hey, beautiful, hurry up! I gotta drive all the way to Dallas today," one of the friendly men called out.

"You're crazy, Joe, y' know that? Dallas is too far for one day. And besides, there's snow down on Raton Pass," she said as she put on her apron and waved to Mac Devine, who was pouring pancakes on the griddle.

"Makes no difference, honey. That's where the money is. If I don't deliver any lettuce, I don't get any lettuce."

She shook her head but smiled. Truck drivers were easier to deal with in the morning, so she was glad she had the early shift. The light banter reflected their eagerness to get into the day's work. At night some of them had a different tone to their remarks.

Soon the diner was filled with hungry men and several women. Some women drove with their husbands, and some even drove by themselves. Janice admired their independence, though she was glad to have a job that kept her home with Billy. She didn't make much money as a waitress, but she believed her hard work would one day make things better for the two of them.

Right now she had to hurry as she delivered stacks of pancakes, eggs of various descriptions, bacon, sausage, extra butter and syrup, and lots of coffee.

Every morning it was the same. She had only a few quiet minutes between home and work. Then she felt as though she had been pulled into a tornado. For over two hours she served hungry people—mostly truckers, some salesmen, a few farmers and ranchers, and once in a while some vacationers on their way to the mountains. By 7:30 the furor had died down, and she had her own cup of coffee and some of Mac's delicious Texas toast.

Mac was the cook and owner of the diner. He managed the early shift, and his wife, Gracie, managed the late one. They claimed that was the only way they could stand to be married to each other. But Janice could see the deep love between them— a love she admired and envied because of her own broken marriage.

Gracie was large and loud and could outshout any trucker, but her heart was big too, and a permanent smile was etched into the wrinkles of her face. Mac was quieter, a generous man who stood by his friends in time of need. Disappointment and adversity had created a sensitivity in this couple toward the hurts of others.

Their diner was small, but it served as an oasis to many lonely, night-driving truckers who wanted a warmer atmosphere than they could find a little farther north in the larger restaurants in Pueblo. And the diner provided a living for Janice and her son, just as it had for a succession of high school girls through the years. It was a good place to be.

Janice finished her brief breakfast, set her second cup of coffee under the counter, and started checking salt and pepper shakers, sugar and creamer packets, and ketchup bottles.

Soon Billy came in for his breakfast, grabbing toast and jelly and ignoring the plate of eggs Mac offered.

"Billy!" his mother scolded.

"Okay, gimme a banana too. Fruit is supposed to be healthy." He grinned as only an adolescent boy can. "Please," he added, his blue eyes sparkling.

His boyish grin won her over as usual, and he hurried out the door to catch the school bus, eating the banana as he went. She watched him, unaware of the proud, maternal glow that lit her face.

"Some kid, eh, Janice?" Mac said.

"Yeah, Mac, some kid. Listen, he'll be thirteen next summer. I've almost got a teenager on my hands!"

"I still say he looks like your kid brother," the old man teased.

"Right," she drawled as she wiped down the counter. She hurried over to the stack of dishes in the kitchen, working quickly to finish before the "farmers' union" arrived for their midmorning coffee break. That was the name she and Mac had given the group of local men who met at the diner every weekday morning except during planting and harvesttime. The men discussed politics, crops, and the latest gossip while they enjoyed Mac's delicious homemade sweet rolls and breads.

"Hey, Jan," Mac said as he worked on his pastries, "I forgot to tell you—Gracie said some guy was here to see you last night."

"Right," she said. They were always trying to be matchmakers for her.

"No, I mean it. A good-looking guy. Tall—a real *dreamboat*," he said, mocking his wife's high-pitched voice on the last word.

"I don't know any tall, good-looking guy who isn't married. Besides, you know truck drivers don't interest me."

"Gracie said he wasn't no trucker. Real classy guy. Drove a fancy sports car."

Janice puzzled over that for a moment, then decided, "It must have been an insurance salesman. You know, trying to sell me something for Billy."

"I dunno, Jan."

"Well, what did Gracie tell him?" she asked.

"Told him you'd be workin' here today and that you get off at 2. He said he'd be back."

"Oh, that's just great. Some stranger comes along and Gracie dishes out my private life on a platter," Janice mumbled.

"Well, she's a sucker for a pretty face. I guess he just got to her."

"Or she's matchmaking again," Janice said as she dried the last cup and placed it under the counter.

She acted unconcerned, even flippant. But fear and anger churned in her mind the rest of the morning. She kept telling herself it couldn't be Bill—he'd never find her. She had gone too far away, and she'd told no one back home where she was. Indeed, there was no one to tell, except her alcoholic mother who was surely dead by now.

By noon she had bungled several orders and spilled two glasses of cola.

Get ahold of yourself, girl, she scolded inwardly. *It can't be him. It can't be!*

Lunch cleanup kept her hands busy but not her mind. She frequently glanced at the wall clock and then at the front window as 2 o'clock drew closer.

Precisely at 2 a bright-red sports car pulled up, and Bill got out.

Bill! It really was him! Janice tried to will her legs to run out the back door, but they refused to obey the command.

He came into the diner, took off his mirrored sunglasses, looked at her, and smiled.

"Hello, Janice," he said softly.

"I don't believe my eyes! . . . Buck Mason!" Mac said from the other end of the counter. "Buck Mason in *my* diner!" The usually quiet man began to babble. "I saw you on TV Sunday. What a passer! You're gonna set a world's record this season for sure. Would you like some coffee? Sit down. Janice, get the man whatever he wants!"

"No, thanks," Bill said, smiling at Mac. His name was Bill, but he went by the nickname Buck. "I just want to talk to Janice." He turned back to her. "Are you off now?"

"Oh, sure, she's off. I can handle things till the other girl gets here. Janice, you go on now. My, my, just wait till I tell Gracie who Janice's visitor turned out to be. That woman never watches anything but soap operas. Didn't even know the greatest quarterback of the decade when she saw him."

Janice and Bill were not even listening to him.

As Janice looked at Bill, the woman in her could not fail to be impressed by his incredible good looks: a strong, handsome face with ice-blue eyes, jet-black hair, a tall, tan, muscular body clothed in very fashionable designer jeans and a knit sports shirt. She started to brush a few loose hairs back from her face but resisted that self-conscious gesture. Let him see her as she was.

Though she was recovering from the initial shock, she did not know what she felt or what she ought to feel. All the anger of all the years gone by seemed drained right out of her. She wanted to be angry. She wanted to scream at him to get out of her life. So often when times had been hard for her and Billy, she had cursed him in her heart. Now she just felt numb. What could he possibly want from her after all this time?

She took off her apron and shoved it into the laundry box under the counter, then pushed past Bill and out the front door. Bill waved to Mac, then followed her out.

"Is there someplace we can talk?" he asked Janice as she stood looking at him, her arms folded defensively.

"My place," she said and turned to walk toward the trailer court.

"Would it be easier to drive?" Bill offered.

Janice whirled around, glared at him, and shot back, "I don't want that thing parked at my house! It would attract too much attention." Only her determination to avoid a scene in front of the diner gave her the strength to turn again and begin the march home.

Bill bit his lower lip and followed her. This was not going to be easy, but he had not expected it to be.

God, help me, he prayed silently.

When he had first stepped into the diner just a few minutes earlier, the struggle in his emotions had rivaled the tension of facing a riptide of 300-pound defensive linemen in the closing minutes of a tie game. Facing this diminutive lady was a task he had only been able to do with the help of prayer and encouragement from older, wiser friends. His and Janice's parting ten years before had been so bitter, so final that he had no idea what to expect from her now.

Seeing her again after all those years, he was struck by the changes. The girlish beauty that had attracted him in tenth grade was now marred by an almost painful thinness. Her complexion, so smooth and creamy back then, was pale now, and dark circles were beginning to appear under her eyes. She was only twenty-eight, the same as him, but she looked older. Most of the women he had known in the intervening years had plenty of time and money to look their best. He knew comparing her to them was unfair. Worse still, he knew he was responsible for the hard times that had diminished her natural beauty so early in life.

Bill followed Janice down the gravel driveway to her trailer. The walk had brought back her self-control, and she was ready to hear what her ex-husband had to say. She unlocked the door and opened it, refusing his offer to open it for her.

"Well, let's have it. What do you want?" She faced him with folded arms once again.

"Could we sit down?" he asked, looking toward the living room.

She shrugged, then turned and walked over to the tattered easy-chair by the front window. He sat on the equally tattered sofa and frowned at the discomfort of it. It seemed that this entire experience was to be one painful reminder after another of the sins of his youth.

"Janice, I had an awful time finding you."

"I never meant for you to find me," she said.

"You've been using your maiden name. Wasn't that hard for Billy?"

"Nobody here knows his last name is Mason," she answered. "Including him."

"Don't worry . . . I didn't come to create problems for you and Billy."

"I'm still waiting to hear why you *did* come."

He signed deeply. Where to begin? What had Dr. Miller suggested?

"Janice, I know this may be hard for you to believe, but I've come to ask you to forgive me for the way I treated you ten years ago. I want you to let me try to make up somehow, just a little, for all you've been deprived of." He spoke haltingly, struggling for the words that would win her trust.

She looked at him wordlessly, steeling herself against those incredible blue eyes and the boyish charm he exuded as he confessed his wrongdoings of the past. She would not let him con her again. At fifteen, it had been easy to be swept off her feet by a tall, dark, handsome guy, especially since she had never known a father's love. But at twenty-eight, after she had learned to put off all kinds of truck drivers and salesmen, she had built up defenses that even Bill's eyes could not break through.

"We don't need nothin' . . . anything." She hastened to correct herself. Bill had lost most of the country drawl they had both spoken as children. She was not going to sound like a hick talking to him. "Billy and I do just fine."

"I don't mean to put you down, but this doesn't exactly look 'fine' to me," Bill said as he looked down the length of the trailer hallway.

"Some people get by with having just a few things because they know what's really important . . . Like taking care of the people they claim to love." She looked at him across the small room, ready for any answer he might have.

"Janice, at sixteen I wasn't ready to be a father . . ."

"And I wasn't ready to be a mother. But I took responsibility for my actions and decided to do the best I could at it. I found out that kids thrive on love. Whatever else you can give them comes in second."

She paused. Her anger was gaining momentum again.

"You know, for two years I gave up everything so you could graduate from high school. You never would have gotten that football scholarship that was your ticket to fame and glory if I hadn't typed your papers and helped you with your homework. And then . . . to find out you'd been cheating on me from the beginning! That showed me a few things, Bill. It taught me never to trust a man again. And it showed me you'd be a lousy father to our son. That's why I left town and tried to lose you forever. You didn't need to come looking for me. I don't need you. Billy doesn't need you! Why . . . why don't you just leave!" Janice quit before he could see the tears that were threatening to come at any moment.

Bill sat looking at his hands for a few minutes. Things were not going the way he'd meant them to. They had gotten off to a bad start.

Finally he said, "I don't blame you for being bitter and angry.

Say whatever you want. I deserve it. But please, just hear me out."

She didn't want to hear another word from this man, but he had listened to her. "Go on," she said reluctantly.

"Well, to begin with, I've changed. I . . . well, I became a Christian a couple of years ago . . ."

Janice broke in. "Oh yeah, I read about that in some magazine. You got religion. That was just two months before you got arrested for drunk driving in New York, right?"

"Uhhh, yeah," he said. She was going to make it rough for him all the way. "But what you have to understand is that being a Christian doesn't make me perfect. It just means I'm forgiven. By God, that is. And after that arrest, the Lord took away my desire for drinking for good. I haven't touched a drop since then."

"Oh, I'm so impressed. You know, Bill, I grew up with a mother who was always drunk—I didn't need any more proof that drinking is stupid."

Bill was quiet again. She had an answer for everything. This discussion was going nowhere.

"Tell me about Billy. Is he doing okay?" he asked.

"He gets good grades in school. He loves computers and football. He thinks you're the greatest quarterback who ever lived. His room is plastered with posters of you, and he reads everything about you he can get his hands on."

Bill could not disguise the amusement this disclosure brought. He felt the tension break that had been rising in his chest during the entire discussion. He chuckled aloud, then suddenly looked at her with concern. "That must be hard for you."

"Why should it be? You're nothing to me. You're just another celebrity out there in the make-believe world." She paused, then added, "He'll outgrow you."

"Would you allow me to see him?" Bill asked nervously. He knew that legally he had the right to see his son, but he had promised himself he would not force the issue.

Janice frowned. It was her turn to study her hands. She wanted to say no, but as she thought about Bill's request, she decided this might be a good way to dig at him again. After all, he did not know about what had happened to Billy. Finally she said, "Sure. He'll be home soon. You can wait here. I'm going to freshen up. I like to look my best when he comes home." She rose and walked through the kitchen and on down the hall.

"May I see his room?" Bill called.

"If he wants you to, he can show you," she answered back down the length of the trailer.

TWO

Bill stared out the living room window, anxious for his first glimpse of his son in ten years. How would Billy react? Would he realize that Bill was the father who had deserted him? Probably not. Janice had said the boy idolized him. That was a bittersweet thought.

Time passed slowly. Bill sat back and studied the room. In addition to the couch and chair, there was a small black-and-white television on a wooden box. The box was covered with a brightly colored scarf to hide its ugliness. A much-used coffee table sat in front of the couch. On it sat a clay something-or-other, obviously made by a child and adorned with painted flowers and the word MOM in bold letters.

Carefully sewn cross-stitch samplers hung on the walls in attractive arrangements, and faded drapes were pulled back from the windows. Numerous houseplants sat here and there in coffee cans or clay pots, and a few tiny, ceramic animals peeked out from behind the leaves.

The room was shabby, but it was neat and clean, as was the kitchen that adjoined it, separated only by a counter that extended halfway across the room. Flowered contact paper on the old refrigerator and on the cupboards brightened the room. Janice had worked hard to make this old trailer a pleasant place for their son to grow up, just as she had worked to make their small apartment an attractive home so many years ago.

Bill remembered her girlish excitement each day when he

came home from afterschool football practice. Billy was clean, she was freshened up, and the apartment was spotless. She never questioned him when he was late, nor when he claimed to have worked overtime at the grocery store where he had a part-time job. Her trust had made it all too easy to have other girlfriends without getting caught.

Hazy memories of the puppy love he had felt for her before they married came to mind. Unlike the girls who gave him what he wanted in return for a chance to wear his letter jacket, Janice never asked for anything. She just wanted to love him and take care of him. News that she was pregnant was delivered to him with a sweet trust that he would take care of her. Bill shuddered when he remembered suggesting abortion. She cried bitterly, and he was overwhelmed with a desire to protect her. They convinced their parents they could make a good home for the baby. Married at sixteen during the summer before his junior year in high school, parents a few months later, they were divorced by graduation. He left their hometown that summer to play football at a major university.

Bill thought back for a moment about his small son. He had been a cute baby, but fatherhood had always seemed unreal to Bill. It almost felt like when he was a child and some girl got him to play dolls. When the game was over, they put the dolls away and forgot them. At eighteen, with a promising future ahead of him, he simply forgot the little black-haired toddler who was just starting to call him Daddy.

Bill's reverie was interrupted as his eyes began to focus on the boyish form coming down the road. He frowned. Something was wrong with this picture! This poor kid limping on an obviously too short left leg could not be Billy! Yet, it was undeniable. The boy looked so much like Bill.

Janice walked into the room just in time to see Bill rise from the couch and stare with his mouth open at the shocking sight. She felt a surge of satisfaction as she watched him struggle to overcome the tears springing to his eyes.

"God, help me . . . Janice, what happened to him?" he whispered hoarsely. "When did it happen?"

"Two years ago. He was climbing on a railroad bridge with some other boys. He fell twenty feet and was lucky to just break his leg. It healed shorter than the other one because he grew more than the doctors expected while he was in the cast."

Janice enjoyed his anguish for a moment, then became alarmed. "Listen, Mr. Christian, you'd better get your act together. It would tear him up to see his hero crying and feeling sorry for him. Go in the bathroom and either get your emotions under control or sneak out the back door. You hear?"

Bill shook his head as if trying to awake from a sudden nightmare, then stumbled down the short hallway to search for the bathroom.

Fortunately, he had time to recover because Billy had stopped to play with a neighbor's German shepherd who greeted him every day after school. The boy dropped his book bag and knelt down to pet the dog, who seemed to wag all over in delight. Finally, to free himself from the friendly attention, Billy picked up a stick and threw it, and the lively dog ran to fetch it.

Billy was breathless as he came into the trailer. "Hey, Mom, did you see that awesome Camaro parked in front of the diner today? Man, what wheels! I gotta get me one of them when I'm sixteen. *Brmmmmm!*" He imitated the sound of a race car's screaming engine at top speed. "I wonder who it belongs to."

"It belongs to our visitor, Billy." Janice tried to sound as casual as possible. Bill was just returning to the kitchen as she spoke.

Billy's mouth gaped. "Wow," he said softly. "Wow! Oh, man—Buck Mason in my house! I don't believe it! Wait till I tell the guys at school. Mr. Mason, can I have your autograph? I've got a picture of you. I'll go get it. Please don't leave yet." He started down the hall toward his room.

"I'm not leaving, Billy. I'd like to visit with you for a while." Bill struggled to keep the emotion out of his voice. "Let's sit in the living room."

"Oh, yeah. This is cool, Mom. Wow! Will you sign my football, Mr. Mason? I'll never use it again. Wow, Mr. Mason. I never miss a Mavericks game when they're on TV. You were great last week. Mr. Mac says you're gonna set a passing record this year for sure."

Bill chuckled. Billy's boyish enthusiasm, like that of hundreds of other boys who idolized him, warmed his heart and settled his churning emotions. "Please call me Buck," he said. He sat on the couch and motioned to his son to join him.

"Wow . . . Can I, Mom?" Billy pleaded. He plopped on the couch next to his hero.

"Yes, you may," she answered. She sat in the easy-chair to monitor their conversation. Why had she failed to make Bill promise not to tell Billy who he was? What if he . . . ?

"What are you doing here, Mr. Mason—I mean, Buck?" Billy's eyes sparkled with excitement.

"Uh, well, your mother and I . . ."

"We went to the same high school," she interrupted.

"Really, Mom? How come you never told me that? Oh, I guess you're older, huh, Mom?" Billy blurted. "He came along later, right?"

Janice glared at Bill, who bit his lower lip and looked down. "I was never sure he was the same person," she said. "Besides, I hate name-droppers."

"Did you know my dad, Buck?" Billy asked.

Bill glanced quickly at Janice.

"He was killed in an Army accident when I was a baby," Billy chattered on. "I've got the medals he won, and an Army commendation letter. I guess he was really a great guy. Did you know Pete Griffin?" Billy studied Buck Mason's face eagerly for confirmation that his father had indeed been a hero.

"Yeah," Bill said hesitantly. "Yeah, I knew Pete. We played football together in high school. He was a little older. And he was a great guy, Billy."

Billy beamed happily, and Bill patted his son's shoulder. He felt a twinge of jealousy that someone else held that special place of respect in Billy's heart. But Bill knew he did not deserve that place. At least, not yet.

Bill glanced at Janice again. He had to admire her skill in creating a good role model for Billy. She could have taught their son to hate him, but she hadn't. As he looked at her, he noticed she had loosened her hair. It fell becomingly around her shoulders, giving her face a softer look. With reluctance, he turned his eyes back to Billy, who began to chatter about football.

Bill and Billy hashed over the previous Sunday's game, which the Mavericks had won in the last moments because of a sensational pass Bill had fired to his top receiver. Bill was impressed with his son's knowledge of the game. And as they talked, he was also amazed at how much Billy looked like him. It was almost like looking into a mirror of the past to see his son's bright, blue eyes and shaggy, black hair.

After a while Janice broke into their animated conversation. "Billy, you have some things to do."

Billy looked at the clock on the kitchen wall. "Oh-oh, I'd better hurry. Hey, Buck, will you be here long? It's been great to talk with you."

"I have to go back tomorrow night. Since we don't have a game this weekend, I was able to take these two days off to come down and see you."

"You mean you came just to see us?"

"Billy, you really have to go. Mrs. Anderson and Mrs. Walters depend on you," Janice interrupted quickly.

"Could I take you two to dinner?" Bill put in.

"Wow! Sure!" Billy said. "I mean, can we, Mom?"

Janice stiffened. This was not a good idea. "I . . . I don't know. I have to get to bed early."

"But, Mom, you don't work tomorrow. It's Saturday."

"I have things to do," she said crossly. Then, seeing his look of disappointment, she added reluctantly, "But you may go."

"Wow! That's great! Thanks, Mom. Thanks, Buck." He

hurried off in his uneven gait to do chores for the two elderly widows in the trailer court.

Janice started to leave Bill alone in the living room, but he stopped her.

"Would you answer some questions? Please?" he said.

She shrugged and sat back down, arms folded.

"I can't believe that nothing could be done for Billy's leg. The medical profession has come up with some amazing things. If they can transplant a heart, they can fix a kid's leg."

"Where do you think I'd get the money to pay for it? I could never afford insurance. I'm still paying for the weeks he was in the hospital when he had the accident. His leg was almost torn off," she said bitterly.

Bill winced. "I don't understand why you didn't call me when it happened. Surely at a time like that you could have put aside your pride . . ." He regretted the word immediately.

"Oh, don't think I didn't consider it," Janice said. "When Billy was in surgery, I borrowed a quarter and went to call you. The phone was being used, so I picked up a magazine to keep my mind occupied. There was a picture of you in it with your arms around a beautiful actress in a low-cut dress and a toothpaste smile. I needed that reminder to know that there's nobody Billy and I can count on but each other. Like I said before, we don't need you."

Bill closed his eyes and groaned. "Janice," he said, "there's no way to tell you how sorry I am. I realize now that when I came here I hoped to put a Band-aid on the wounds of the past. I should have known how deep they are. Please forgive me. Please let me do something!"

"Just take Billy out for a hamburger. No, make it pizza. That's one thing we don't make at the diner. Then maybe a movie. Then get out of here. That will be enough to keep him walking two feet off the ground for months—at least until football season is over and he starts reading up on his favorite basketball hero."

Bill sat on the edge of the couch and glared at her. "If you think I'm just going back to my team and forget my son, you're crazy. I have plenty of money, and I'm going to see to it he gets that leg fixed."

"And then I suppose you'll find a way to bring him to live with you. You have so much more to offer him than I do. What kid could resist that? No! I won't let you do it!" She gripped the arms of her chair.

"Janice, if I have to go to court to get custody to get his leg fixed, I will!"

"Is that the way Christians do things? Using all your money and influence to steal my son away from me? You don't have a case. I've been a good mother, and I have character witnesses to prove it." She returned his angry glare.

But her last remarks had broken his anger. He put his head in his hands in frustration. No matter what he said to her, it came out wrong. He never lost control of himself in a football game, no matter how rough it got. But with Janice, he was completely losing control of his temper. What kind of Christian testimony was that?

After a moment of tense silence, he said, "Look, I'm sorry I said that. I know you're a good mother. I'm honestly not trying to hurt you. But we have to work something out for Billy's sake. You can tell him it's out of Christian love that I want to help him."

"Let me tell you about 'Christian love.' When Billy was lying there in the hospital, some 'loving' ladies from a local church decided to make us their charity project, so they took turns sitting with me. I overheard one of them say I was a cheap little waitress in a trashy diner." Janice bit back the angry tears as she recalled the nightmare two years before.

"They assumed that because I was a single parent I was a divorcée and therefore had low moral character. I managed to slip in that my late husband had died an Army hero, and that sure changed their tune. They couldn't be nice enough then. But I told them to forget it. My friends, Mac and Gracie, got me through Billy's ordeal, and their help came from their hearts, not because I was a Sunday school project."

"Janice, I know some Christians are like that. We're human. We make mistakes. But I'm really trying to be what Jesus Christ wants me to be. I'm new at it, but every day God shows me ways to be more like Him. He's the One you need to look at." Bill finally felt that he had said something right.

But Janice simply asked, "Is this when you tell me I need to be saved?" She enjoyed his startled look for a moment, then added, "Billy watched you on TV with some preacher one time. He asked me what it meant to be saved. I told him it was for people who couldn't do the right thing without help. As for Billy and me, we don't need it. Doing good just comes naturally. Nobody makes him do chores for those elderly widows. It was his own idea. Gracie and Mac believe in God, and they adopt everybody who comes along. What do they need to be saved from?"

From hell, that's what! he thought. But he did not trust himself to answer her aloud.

Alone once more after Janice went to her room, Bill wondered if he was the right person to witness to her. She had always been a good person. Her only mistake had been in loving him too much and trusting him too much.

He, on the other hand, had led a self-centered life. Then, just two years ago, his teammate, Scott Lansing, had taken him to a Fellowship of Christian Athletes meeting. The speaker was a former football star whom Bill admired. What he said made good sense to Bill, and that night he trusted Jesus Christ as his own Savior. He gradually allowed the Lord to remove drinking, sexual immorality, and drugs from his life and to replace them with Himself.

Last summer, before the beginning of workouts for the new football season, Scott had taken Bill to a Christian growth seminar. There he learned about his responsibility to clear up his past before he could grow into spiritual maturity. The more he learned, the more he realized how selfish his life had been. It wasn't easy to face all that, but he had no desire to turn back now.

THREE

By the time Billy returned from his labors of love, Janice had extracted a promise from Bill that he would not tell Billy about their relationship. That secret weighed heavily on him.

Billy washed up and put on his best jeans. Janice always managed to give him one good outfit every year. Except for his old sneakers, his appearance was acceptable when Bill took him out for pizza.

Billy examined every detail of the fancy sports car. Bill always ordered the works, so this VIP rental was fully equipped with every possible luxury. Billy selected a compact disk and put it into the player.

"Hey, great! Randy Travis. I like him," Bill said.

"Wow! I bet you know everybody that's anybody," Billy said.

Bill chuckled. "Tell me about school, Billy," he said. "Do you like it?"

"Yeah, it's okay. I like geography 'cause I want to travel and take my mom with me. She never gets to go anywhere. I hate English, especially compositions. I really like computer class. And . . ." He looked at Bill, trying to decide whether to share his secret. Yes, Buck could be trusted. "And I like cooking class, too."

Bill nodded his approval. "Sounds like you're on the right track. Trust me—as a bachelor, there are times I wish I had paid attention to more than the girls in cooking class."

Billy beamed. Then he glanced down at his leg.

"Y' know, I wasn't born this way," he said, tapping his left knee.

Bill swallowed hard. "Oh?" he said.

"Naw. I had an accident. Two years ago. But it's okay. I get around all right."

"I'm sure you do, Billy." Bill stifled the urge to tell his son he had every intention of seeing that his leg was repaired.

After dinner they drove to a theater where a popular action-adventure movie was playing. The next show wouldn't begin for an hour, so Bill steered Billy across the street to a shoe store.

"Which of these do you like best?" he asked the boy as they checked out the window display.

"All the guys at school wear cowboy boots. 'Course, most of them are cowboys. But Mom can't afford to get me boots, so sneakers are okay."

"Do you think your mom would mind if I bought you a pair of boots?" Bill asked.

"Man, would you? Oh, man, that would be cool. She lets Mac buy me stuff sometimes. Would you?"

Bill answered by taking the boy into the store and ordering the best brand available in Billy's size. A smiling boy and his father marched across the street to the movie theater. Bill felt an exciting new power, a new joy he'd never experienced, in the simple act of providing a basic need for his son. He wanted more of this. Much more. Would Janice stand in his way?

After the movie, they bought ice cream cones at the parlor next door, though they had already had pizza and popcorn. "Growing boys like us need a lot of fuel," Bill said.

"Right, Buck!" Billy agreed.

Bill reluctantly drove back to the trailer court a few miles south of Pueblo. Janice met them at the door, arms folded.

"Mom, we had a great time. I wish you had come along with us. We saw *Blazer Man*. It was cool. We had pizza, popcorn, and ice cream. Man, I'm about to bust! And look—Buck bought me some boots. I can keep them, can't I?"

"What can I say? You've already worn them," she said. Noting his sheepish look, she added, "They look nice, honey. Now you go on to bed."

"Mom, can Buck come throw the football around with me tomorrow? I mean, would you, Buck?" Billy asked, his eyes bright with excitement.

"Don't you think you've taken about all the time he can spare?" Janice said, glaring at Bill.

"No. He said he's off till tomorrow night, right, Buck?" Billy said.

Bill smiled. "Yeah. I'd love to come over. Janice?"

Janice felt her heart skip a beat as he looked at her. He looked just like Billy. The same boyish smile that always made her give in to Billy was making her go along with Bill. She looked down. "Just don't come too early. We sleep in on Saturday to catch up on our rest."

"All right!" Bill and Billy burst out in unison, giving each other a thumbs-up at the same time, then laughing together in happy camaraderie.

Tears of jealousy burned Janice's eyes, but the others didn't notice. "Now you get to bed, Billy," she said.

"Okay, Mom. Good night. Good night, Buck. Thanks for the boots! See you tomorrow." Billy left the room without kissing his mother good night.

Bill treasured his last look at his son. "See you tomorrow," he said.

As the boy limped down the short hallway to his room, Janice turned to Bill, and he could see her tears. His heart stirred, and he wanted to take her into his arms and comfort her. She looked so vulnerable, so terribly threatened. He began to take a step closer, but she tilted her head up defiantly.

"I can't lock the door until you go out," she said.

"Sorry. Well, good night," he said as he stepped out. "And . . . thanks, Janice."

The words went unheard as she shut the door in his face.

Janice started down the hallway, then decided to claim her good-night kiss from Billy. As she tapped on his door, it swung open. Billy sat on his bed examining his left calf where a raw spot had developed in the short time he had worn the cowboy boots.

"I guess I'm not supposed to wear these." He held the offending boot and traced the design across the toe with his finger.

Janice sighed. Why had Bill done this? And if he had to do it, why didn't he get sneakers?

"Oh, we can figure something out," she said. "Supposedly leather softens up to fit you. Besides, some long socks will help. Cheer up, honey."

"Mom, we had a great time. He really likes me," Billy said. He glanced up at the posters on his wall. Most of them were of Buck Mason in football gear, either passing or posing. One action shot had won an award for the photographer and had become a popular poster for thousands of young boys like Billy.

"Do you think he'd write to me after he leaves?"

"Oh, you never can tell about people like that," she said. "You don't want to impose on him."

Billy sighed. "Yeah, I guess not."

While they talked, Janice walked into the bathroom for some salve for Billy's leg. It had been some time since she had seen the faded scars from his accident, and she tried not to wince as her fingers touched them. Now that he was an adolescent his modesty had increased. But at least he still let her tuck him in and kiss him good night.

She lay on her bed for a long while that night, thinking about all that day's happenings. While Bill and Billy were out, she had dug out an old Bible she had been given many years before at a small church back in Alabama. As a youngster she had gone to Sunday school for two years with a neighbor. It had been a welcome relief from her dreary life at home. Her father had abandoned them before she could remember, and her mother was an alcoholic. Janice and her brother Pete had raised themselves. Pete was older than Janice and had been too busy to help her through her growing-up trials, having plenty of his own. And yet, when he was killed in the Army, she felt the loss desperately.

The Bible had been some comfort to her at first, but she did not really understand it. The dim light that had begun to dawn in her soul during those few childhood Sunday school days later faded, and she found herself asking questions the Good Book did not seem to answer. If she had been a good wife, why had Bill cheated on her? If Pete had been a good man and a hero, why did he die in a meaningless battle drill? Didn't the Bible say the righteous were supposed to prosper?

She believed God existed, but she doubted He was much interested in her. She figured that at the end of life He would weigh her good deeds against her bad ones, and she was determined to make sure there would be more good ones. Over the years she had worked hard at being kind and honest, and she'd taught Billy to do the same.

Billy had a gentle disposition, and he loved animals and old people. It was not difficult to raise him. His accident had been a hard way of learning not to follow the crowd, and yet he accepted his limitations bravely and without self-pity or malice.

Janice found herself examining their life and character. Was there any fault in them? No, she thought, they were okay. She had deliberately chosen to live alone, to be moral, to turn down dates with men who came to the diner—even the nice ones. The few men her mother had brought home had disgusted her, and she would not risk losing Billy's respect in the same way.

To fill the gaps in their life, she had spent her free time reading good literature. Listening to an English class on public television, she had corrected her poor grammar. Though she did not flaunt her newfound skill at the diner, she did feel comfortable talking to the well-educated staff at the public library. After much study and earning her General Equivalency Diploma, she had planned to begin classes at the local college. But then Billy had his accident. She was still paying the hospital bill.

Now her only dream was to teach Billy to fend for himself and to get him educated somehow.

Janice tossed about in her bed. What right did Bill have coming around like this—and so suddenly, after so many years? What was this "forgiveness" he was talking about? Didn't he know that *nothing* could repair the damage he'd done? Men were all the same—her father, the truck drivers, Bill. But maybe somehow she could help Billy be different.

While Bill had entertained Billy at the movie, Janice had searched her old Bible for some of the contradictions she had once seen there. She planned to throw them in Bill's Christian face. But instead, she began reading at the beginning and was soon caught up in the stories, reading them like a novel. The time slipped away, and before she knew it father and son were home, and she quickly hid the Bible before Bill could see it.

Bill returned to his motel thankful the Lord had kept fans away during this emotionally exhausting evening. In this part of southern Colorado, he'd figured there would be places where people wouldn't know who he was, and he'd prayed that God would direct him to those places. The man at the diner had worried him, but since nothing had come of it, Bill dismissed it from his mind.

He flung himself on the bed and lay studying the ceiling for a while, sorting out his thoughts. When he had attended the Christian growth seminar, he had learned that an important step in becoming a mature Christian involves clearing up one's past. For him, that meant setting things straight with his ex-wife and son. He was doing the right thing to seek Janice's forgiveness, but she didn't seem interested in granting it. But what did he expect from her? Instant acceptance? For a brief moment he wished she had happily remarried. That would have solved everything. Then he regretted the thought and prayed for forgiveness. So what was his next step? Did he just want to throw some money her way, buy a few things for the kid, and return free and clear to the carefree life he had been living? He pondered her insistence that they keep their relationship a secret from Billy. It was all so complicated.

When he had first accepted Jesus Christ as his Savior, he had been following the lead of men he knew and respected. As he began to live as a Christian, however, he began to remember many of his youthful escapades and realized how deeply sinful he had been. He then changed his habits and some of his friends. He had spent the two years since his salvation seeking to please God and to share God's love with others.

Now he had come to Colorado to seek Janice's forgiveness and had come face to face with his son, Billy. How could he have forgotten his son during the intervening years? Maybe if he had been there, Billy wouldn't have had the accident. He tossed restlessly on his bed as waves of guilt washed over him.

Finally he reached for the phone and dialed his pastor. Dr. Miller had promised to be at home in Los Angeles that evening.

He told the pastor about the day's events, including Janice's anger and his own guilt. "How am I going to get this thing settled, Doc?" he said.

"You have to give it time, Buck. You have to consider how this looks to Janice. The bitterness has been there for ten years. It will take time to show her that you really want to help. Of course she feels threatened."

"Threatened? She was like a brick wall," Bill said.

Dr. Miller chuckled. "Now, Buck, you've admitted to me more than once that women have always spoiled you rotten. In fact, you usually get your way in most things, don't you?"

Bill muttered a noncommittal "Hmmm."

"Maybe the Lord has a lesson in patience for you in this situation," the pastor continued. "I have an idea. Why don't you take her some flowers when you go see her tomorrow? See if that will soften her up."

"Flowers. Yeah, that's a good idea. Thanks, Doc."

"I'll keep you in prayer, Buck. Let me know how things transpire."

Despite the encouragement, Bill slept fitfully that night. Dr. Miller was right. Women had always pampered him. He should not want Janice to merely be charmed by him. He should be praying for her to come to Christ. Her salvation and Billy's should be his primary goal. He had his work cut out for him. *O God of heaven, help me . . . show me the way.*

FOUR

Billy rose early to finish his Saturday chores so they wouldn't interfere with the day's adventure. Imagine—playing football with Buck Mason! He dug the movie ticket stub out of his jeans pocket to be sure last night had not been a dream, then proudly tacked it onto the wall. He was afraid he would again forget to get Buck's autograph, so he asked his mother to remind him.

As for Janice, she quickly dusted and swept the already clean house, then told Billy she would be at the diner if she needed her. She had slept badly and woke up with the gnawing fear that Bill would somehow manage to get custody of Billy. She aimed to get Mac and Gracie on her side, though she knew Mac was a fan of Bill's—or Buck's, as Mac knew him. Would Mac's friendship with her take supremacy over his idol-worship? She scolded herself for doubting, but she doubted nevertheless.

Mac and Gracie claimed Saturday and Sunday mornings for themselves. The rest of the time, one of them was sure to be in the diner, with their adjoining apartment making it easy for them to trade off shifts. They had several high school girls who competently filled in for them when needed.

When Janice appeared at their back door, her expression alarmed them.

"Why, honey, come on in," Gracie said. "What brings you out on Saturday morning?"

"Janice, that was Buck Mason who came to see you yesterday, wasn't it? Tell Gracie it was," Mac urged.

Janice nodded, then flung herself into Gracie's outstretched arms and wept.

"Well, I'll be," Mac said.

Gracie added, "I told you this means trouble for her and Billy. Now ain't you glad I kept you from blabbing all over about him?"

"Well, I didn't know . . ."

"Folks got a right to secrets, Mac. We got a few of our own, remember?" Gracie said. "Now, Janice honey, you just talk when you're ready."

Janice told them her story, starting with the day in tenth grade when Bill had selected her above all the wealthier, more popular girls to be his special one. She had felt like Cinderella and had given her all to the relationship. She went on to tell them about the painful divorce and her running away to Colorado.

"This is as far as I could buy a bus ticket for. If you all hadn't been here, I don't know what Billy and I would have done. I just had to get to somewhere where nobody could find us."

"My goodness, girl," Mac said, "I thought Buck Mason was different from the pack . . . And all this time Billy making do without a pa."

"What if he tries to take Billy away?" Janice asked through her tears.

"I'll tell you what, honey," Gracie said, "we're in this together, and we won't let that happen."

"That's right," Mac grunted. "We'll fight it together."

"But what if Billy wants to go live with Bill after he finds out he's his father?" Janice inquired.

"Oh, now listen, honey," Gracie said, patting Janice's hand, "a good boy like Billy don't just up and leave his mama. Not when she's been as good to him as you have."

"Come on, sis," Mac said, "it's gonna be okay. Cheer up now."

Janice sniffed back her tears. "Thanks. I don't know what I'd do without you guys. You're the only people in this world I've ever been able to trust."

"And we ain't gonna let you down this time neither," Mac said.

Bill arrived at the trailer at just after 10 o'clock. Billy was waiting with his old, battered football in hand. But Bill had brought a new football in one hand and a dozen pink roses in the other. He had meant to buy red ones, but as he awoke that morning he seemed to remember that Janice preferred pink. He hoped he was right.

"Wow!" Billy said. "How did you know my mom likes pink? Here, let me find a jar." He dug around under the kitchen sink, pulled out an empty coffee can, and filled it with water. He arranged the flowers skillfully.

"Hey, you do that pretty well," Bill said.

"Aw, nothing to it. When I was a kid I was always bringing Mom wildflowers. She showed me how to fix them like in the magazines."

"Where is your mom?" Bill asked.

"She had to go over to Mac and Gracie's. We can leave anytime. It's okay." Billy finished arranging the flowers and picked up the new football, gripping it for a throw.

Bill glanced out the front window and frowned. He had hoped to see her. But at least he had been right about the pink roses. As he had read his Bible that morning, he felt God's assurance that things would go well today. Patience, Dr. Miller had said last night. Right now, Bill was happy just to be with his son.

At Billy's direction, they drove several miles south of the trailer court to the consolidated school he attended. The football field gave them plenty of room to play.

In spite of his shorter leg, Billy ran enthusiastically, though with an uneven gait. He wore his sneakers and hoped Buck would not ask about the boots.

Bill was not looking at Billy's shoes, however. He was watching with great pride as Billy hurled the football to him with speed and accuracy. He had inherited his father's arm.

After a while, several other boys and girls arrived for their usual Saturday play at the schoolyard. When word got around that Buck Mason of the Los Angeles Mavericks was there, he and Billy were surrounded by eager players wanting to get in on the action.

Bill wanted to spend the time only with his son, but Billy enjoyed the attention his guest was getting. When the group took a break from football, Bill signed autographs on footballs, baseballs, T-shirts, a cast on a broken arm, and numerous scraps of paper retrieved from the dumpster beside the cafeteria.

After another short game, Bill pulled Billy away from the group and drove north into Pueblo.

"What do you want for lunch, Billy?"

"Hey, how about the Taco House? I can eat half a dozen tacos," Billy answered.

"Sounds good," Bill said.

They ordered at the drive-through, then drove to a park to eat.

"Billy, there's something I want to talk to you about," Bill said.

Billy looked up from his lunch with interest.

"Billy, what do you know about God?" *Oh, no. That was the wrong way to start,* he thought. Still, if he didn't jump right in . . .

Billy appeared confused by the question, so Bill tried again.

"What I mean is, do you know that God loves you very much?"

"I guess so," Billy said. "I always think of God as being real far away . . . Up in heaven. That's where my dad is. Someday I'll get to see him, I guess." He thought for a moment, then added, "If I'm good enough."

"Do you think you can be good enough to get to heaven? I mean, since God made heaven perfect, only perfect people can be there. Even if you had just one small flaw, it would keep you out," Bill said.

Billy looked down with concern. "Do you think God will keep me out because of my leg?"

"No, Billy. That's not the kind of perfect I'm talking about. I'm talking about what's in your heart . . . your thoughts. Everything we do is because of what we think; so if we think bad things, sooner or later we'll *do* bad things."

Billy nodded as he bit into his fourth taco. "That makes sense," he said, catching a bit of falling lettuce. "I guess it's important to keep thinking good thoughts. Hey, can we go to the civic center? My science teacher says they're having an electronics and computer show there all this weekend. I really want to see it."

Bill had noticed that his son didn't stay on any subject except computers or football for more than a few minutes; so he decided to get back to spiritual things later. The day passed quickly, however, with a great deal of time being spent discussing the various models of home computers. Bill made a mental note about the one he would buy for Billy's Christmas present. If he brought it without asking, maybe Janice wouldn't make him take it back.

"I'd better get you home, Billy," Bill said, glancing at his watch. "It's getting late. Your mother might be worried."

Billy sighed and nodded. "Yeah, I guess you're right." Then he brightened. "Hey, will you stay for supper? Mom always told me I can invite my friends whenever I want."

"I'd like that," Bill said. He tried to picture Janice's reaction to this surprise. He found himself looking forward to seeing her again.

When Janice went home that morning, she felt better at having someone to share her problems with. She often wondered how she and Billy would have made it without Mac and Gracie. Today she carried home a large plate full of leftover meatloaf from the diner. And they always gave Billy all the milk he could drink.

As she entered the trailer, the fragrance of the roses attracted her immediate attention. Placing the meatloaf in the refrigerator, she went to the table to examine them. Every rose was perfect . . . And they were pink! *What a lovely surprise*, she thought.

"Wait a minute," she said. "Just what is he trying to do? I know Bill—he must have some ulterior motive."

She scooped up the flowers, went to the door, and tossed them out, can and all. She turned back into the house but immediately regretted her hasty action. What would Billy think? She ran out the door just in time to see the neighbor's dog grab a mouthful of the flowers .

"No! Bad dog!" she yelled as she frantically retrieved the flowers and decorative ferns that lay in the dirt. She hurried back indoors to wash them and return them to the table. The roses had survived, only a little worse for the experience.

As she placed the coffee can on the table, she noticed a tiny envelope with a card inside. It read, "Let's be friends." A smiley face grinned at her from the card, and she almost smiled in return. Not too threatening, she supposed. She would enjoy the flowers but would be on guard at everything Bill did. Maybe he wouldn't try to take Billy, after all.

Emotional exhaustion overcame her, and she lay down to take a nap. It was late in the afternoon when she awoke, and she hurried to freshen up. She brushed her long, light-brown hair and let it fall loosely around her face. Then she looked through her dresser to find an old mascara. It had long ago dried out. Even putting water on the applicator did not make it give out any color. But at least brushing her lashes emphasized their length. She pulled her hair up to the top of her head, then brushed it down again with a frown. Hearing the car door slam outside, she went to the kitchen just as Billy and Bill came in.

"Mom, I brung home a stray. Can I keep him?" Billy teased. It had always been one of their games, and always before she had said, "I'll put another bean in the pot." This time she looked at Bill in confusion. "We're just having leftover meatloaf . . . and turnip greens."

"Turnip greens! Do you know what it's like trying to get turnip greens outside of Alabama? Can I stay?" Bill asked with childish enthusiasm that made Billy laugh.

Janice shrugged. "Go wash up," she said to Billy. She avoided saying yes to Bill, but she did set another place at the table.

Bill leaned over the kitchen counter watching her put the meal on the table. "It's hard to find grits most places, too."

"I wouldn't know," she said under her breath so Billy couldn't hear. "I saw you in a wine commercial once. Looked to me like you were enjoying some mighty fancy food."

"But that was . . ."

"Oh, how could I forget? Before you were a Christian, of course."

Throughout dinner Billy kept the conversation jumping from one topic to another. Bill seemed to enjoy both the food and the company. Janice felt a twinge of jealousy that Bill had been able to take their son to the computer show. She knew how important it was to his science grade. But since she didn't drive, there was no way she could have taken Billy there.

All too soon for Billy, Bill looked at his watch and said, "I have to meet my friend at the airport at 9:30. He's flying me back to L.A. I've had a great day, Billy."

"Me, too, Buck. Thanks for everything. Oh, I left my football in the car," he said as he ran out to retrieve it.

Bill took this chance to tell Janice, "You're a wonderful mother. You've done a great job with Billy. I hope you'll let me help you out . . . And that someday you'll forgive me for hurting you." His eyes gently pleaded for a positive response.

Janice looked down to avoid their appeal. "I told you, we don't need anything."

"Did you ever consider that I was supposed to pay you a hundred dollars a month in child support all this time?" he asked. "Do you realize that comes to twelve thousand dollars for ten years' backpayments?"

Her eyes widened for a moment as she looked back at him. Then she muttered, "I told that judge I didn't want anything, and I still mean it." She looked away again from his intense gaze.

Billy returned with the football. He found a pen in the kitchen drawer and said eagerly, "Buck, will you autograph my football for me?"

Bill put his hand on Billy's shoulder. "Billy, I want you to trust me about something. Please don't ask for my autograph."

Billy frowned, then glanced at his mother, who simply shrugged. "But the kids at school won't believe I know you," he said, his face almost a mirror image of Bill's pained expression.

"The ones we played football with today will tell the others, won't they?"

"Yeah, I guess so," Billy said, staring at the floor.

Bill put his arm around the boy's shoulder. "Look, I'll do something even better, Billy. Here's my card. If you ever need anything or even just want to talk, you call me . . . collect. Okay?" He placed his business card in Billy's hand.

"Do you really mean it?"

"Absolutely!"

Janice frowned at this, but Bill reached for her hand.

"Dear lady, thank you for sharing your fine son with me today. I hope to see you both again soon." He raised her hand to his lips and kissed it in a mock-courtly fashion, winking at Billy as he did so. Billy wrinkled his nose in return.

Janice pulled her hand back and crossed her arms, her eyes cold. "Good-bye," she said. "Don't think it hasn't been fun."

Billy followed Bill out to the car.

"Buck, do you like my mom? I mean . . . do you like her?"

"I like you both a lot, Billy."

There was an awkward pause as Bill savored this last look at his son. Then he tousled Billy's hair, jumped into the car, and drove away. It wasn't until he was halfway to the airport that he realized he had not finished telling Billy about the Lord.

FIVE

The next morning Janice sat drinking coffee with Mac and Gracie. The couple hung on every word as she described the previous evening.

"When he kissed my hand, I wanted to slap him," Janice said loudly. "I would have if Billy hadn't been there. That was so stupid."

Mac tried to hide a chuckle. "Now, Janice, maybe he did get himself straightened out. I've seen it happen before. You might give the man a chance and just see what he wants."

But Gracie scowled. "You can't trust people like that. They use their money to get whatever they want, smiling at you all the while. I don't want him hurting Janice again."

"I still think it would be mighty selfish of Janice if she didn't let Buck do something for his own son," Mac said. "Why, I'd do all I could for the boy if he was mine."

Gracie glared at her husband. "And who's gonna tell Billy this fella's his pa?"

"Hush, woman. I ain't a fool. It's Billy I'm thinking about. He deserves a few good turns in life. If Buck wants to foot the bill to ease his conscience, I say let him do it."

Janice was used to their arguing. But the essence of their conflict mirrored her own inner struggle. She couldn't let her own pride and selfishness stand in the way of Billy's happiness. She had spent the past ten years working to give Billy what she could, and yet Bill could do more in a day than she had done in all that time. What right did she have to stand in the way?

Several days later Billy received a letter from Buck Mason. Buck wrote that he had subscribed to a Christian youth magazine for Billy and hoped he would enjoy it. He included news about several of his teammates Billy had asked about. He reminded Billy to watch the Broncos/Mavericks game the following Sunday.

Billy was a popular seventh-grader at school that week. He often noticed classmates looking at him and talking quietly. Several bolder students asked him how he knew the famous football player. Billy just smiled mysteriously. He didn't tell them he had never gotten a straight answer as to why Buck had suddenly looked up his mother. She was obviously older than Buck, he thought. And they had only been casual acquaintances in high school. Billy began to look at his mother in a new light, trying to figure things out.

By the next Sunday Mac had rented a large-screen television and put it up in the corner of the diner. Billy and Janice came to watch the game, and many neighbors crowded into the place, making it nearly impossible for customers to get served.

The network sports announcer interviewed both starting quarterbacks before the game, asking the usual questions about who was going to do what and what they thought of the opposing team. At the end of his interview Buck Mason waved to the camera and said, "Hello, Billy!"

The diner erupted with applause, and several Denver Broncos fans almost hoped the Mavericks would win just for the boy's sake. People in the area had a soft spot for the injured lad. Some felt silent guilt, knowing their own sons had been on the railroad bridge the day he fell. There had been something suspicious going on, but no one ever mentioned it.

Everything came together for the Mavericks that day. Buck won the coin toss; so his team received the ball first. Scott Lansing caught the kickoff on the Mavericks' ten yard line and ran twenty-five yards. When Buck came in for the first down, it only took him three more plays against the tough Broncos defense and the Mavericks had their first touchdown. Placekicker Jeff Pearson made the extra point. By halftime the score was 28 to 14 in favor of the Mavericks. Billy was wild with excitement. It had always been hard to be a Mavericks fan in the middle of Broncos territory, but he and Mac were finally having their day.

The Broncos came back strong in the second half, but the Mavericks came back stronger. Though the Broncos scored two impressive touchdowns, the Mavericks blocked one of the Broncos' extra point attempts. Also, Buck led the Mavericks to another touchdown and then a last-quarter field goal for good measure. As the cameras panned the crowd, the Los Angeles players and fans went wild in Denver's Mile-High Stadium.

Janice yawned. As far as she was concerned, football players were just little boys in men's bodies. She watched them hop around, carrying the coach off the field and congratulating each other in the locker room. She had been bored with the whole thing by halftime.

A few Broncos fans left the diner in a sour mood, but the good sports among them patted Billy on the back as though he had won the game himself.

That night when Janice tucked Billy in and kissed him good night, he took her hand and asked her to sit on the bed.

"Mom," he said, "do you think I could ever play pro football? I mean, is there any way I could? Naw—not with my bum leg. Even though I can handle the ball with the best of them, this stupid leg would mess me up. I'll never be able to run."

Janice brushed his shaggy hair away from his face. He so rarely discussed his injury. She knew she was hearing his heart's cry.

"Now, Billy, didn't I teach you never to say never? Good little boys—I mean, good big boys like you always get whatever they reach for."

"But my dad was good, and he got killed. You're so good, Mom. The best! But look how hard you have to work. What does it get you?"

"Haven't I always told you that hard work is good for us? If we keep working hard, someday things will get better," she said.

"But how, Mom? How?"

"I don't know, Billy. You just have to have faith."

"Faith in what, Mom?"

The question startled her. "Oh, Billy, I don't know. In life, I guess. In yourself. You just have to keep on trying."

"Oh," he said, sighing. Weariness crept into his voice. "Good night, Mom. I love you."

"I love you, too, Billy."

As the boy turned over to go to sleep, he wondered sleepily if Buck had an answer to his questions.

While the rest of the Mavericks boarded their private airplane to return to Los Angeles, Bill took advantage of being back in Colorado to see Janice and Billy again. He prayed he could convince Janice to accept his offer to pay for Billy's surgery and to agree to see a highly recommended specialist in Denver. This time, however, being more sensitive as to how their neighbors might view his visit, he rented a secondhand pickup truck and dressed in nondescript western garb.

He arrived at the trailer on Monday afternoon shortly before Janice got off work. Waiting in the cab of the pickup, he looked like any cowboy in the area, although a discerning onlooker might recognize him.

Janice, returning home from work, felt her throat tighten when she saw the pickup and especially when she saw who was in it. She was irritated that Bill kept surprising her when she looked her worst. Why couldn't he at least give her a chance to get cleaned up after work?

As she approached the truck, Bill jumped out. "Hi, Janice! It's good to see you." He smiled warmly, and his eyes twinkled.

Janice looked away. She wished he hadn't come, but it was also a struggle to not smile back at him. He looked so handsome! But she knew she would be a fool to trust him again.

"Hi," she answered briefly, brushing past him and going into the trailer.

He followed, undaunted.

Janice plopped into her chair in the living room, and Bill sat on the couch. There was an awkward silence for a few moments.

"Janice . . ."

"Look . . ."

They spoke at the same time, then were silent again.

"Look," Janice began again, "I just want you to know that I've decided to let you help Billy. If you are still willing to pay for the surgery to have his leg fixed, that would be appreciated. It's nice of you to offer."

"That's great, Janice. Just great!" Bill exclaimed. He laughed with relief. All the arguments he'd rehearsed so carefully had turned out to be unnecessary. "Listen, I've been in contact with a friend whose brother is a doctor in Denver—a children's orthopedic surgeon at Children's Hospital. All I have to do is make an appointment whenever it's convenient for you and Billy. He'll take some X-rays, check Billy over, and set a date for the surgery."

"Okay," she said. She looked at her hands, then played with a loose thread on the chair's arm.

Bill could not read anything in her face. He cleared his throat. "Great!" he said after a few moments. "Now, when do we tell Billy?"

"I'll tell him after he does his chores."

Another silence. The soft clatter of the refrigerator motor and the click of the clock as the second hand moved around were the only sounds in the room.

"Could I take you two out to dinner?" Bill asked hesitantly.

"So you don't really like turnip greens and meatloaf?"

"Oh, yeah, I do. But I couldn't invite myself to dinner, could I? Besides, I really would like to take you . . . uh, I mean both of you . . . out." His intense blue eyes sparkled.

Janice gave a slight shrug, glancing up and quickly looking back at her hands.

"Well?" he said.

"Well, what?"

"Will you go out to dinner with me? Or are you having turnip greens for supper tonight?"

"Turnip greens are out of season. The ones we had last week were the last fresh ones of the year. Canned don't taste any good," she added. "By the way, I appreciate you not coming in a fancy car this time. That other one brought some unwanted attention. In fact, we've been getting a lot of stares since you were here before."

"I'm sorry. I didn't mean to—"

"You look right at home in a pickup. Just like a cowboy," she said.

"I'm going to be in a western movie next spring," he said.

Janice rolled her eyes and shook her head.

"Besides, I like pickups. Always have," he added quickly, sorry he had mentioned the movie and hoping Janice didn't think he was rubbing his success in her face.

"I remember when all you wanted was a pickup, a dog, and gravy on your grits."

Bill laughed. "You'd be surprised at how little my tastes have changed."

"Oh, yeah. I'm sure," she said sarcastically. "When did your friends start calling you *Buck?*" She spat the word out.

Bill ignored her tone and answered casually, "When I went to college I was in the Rodeo Club. Everybody had a nickname, and I was Buck. When I started making a name for myself in football, it just stuck. Sports announcers are always looking for something like that to pin on you."

Billy bounded in the door at just that moment, so Janice bit back her sarcastic reply.

"Hey, Buck! What a game yesterday! I was so proud to know you. Mac set up a big-screen TV in the diner, and we all watched you. Man, what a game! That pass in the third quarter . . . Wow!" Billy pantomimed throwing a football.

"Hi, Billy. It's good to see you!" Bill shook the boy's hand warmly and slapped him on the shoulder. With difficulty he refrained from giving his son a bear hug and telling him how much he loved him.

"What are you doing here?" Billy asked. His eyes sparkled as he looked at his hero.

"I just came down to see you since I was back in Colorado. Gotta see my favorite fan every chance I get."

Billy grinned from ear to ear.

Bill decided to take a risk. "I'm taking you and your mom to dinner, so you'd better get your chores done."

"All right!" Billy shouted as he hurried down the hall to change into his grubbies. "I gotta clean Mrs. Walters's refrigerator. She's blind, so she spills stuff a lot. Then I gotta chop kindling wood for Mrs. Anderson's Ben Franklin stove," Billy yelled from his room. He came back into the kitchen just moments later. "It shouldn't take too long. I'll hurry."

"Do a good job though," Bill said.

"I will. Man, that pass was awesome. Sixty yards!" He again pretended to throw a football.

"Hello, Billy," Janice said sheepishly.

"Oh, hi, Mom," Billy said as he rushed out the door.

Janice's shoulders sagged, and tears sprang to her eyes. Her son had hardly even noticed her!

Bill sat back down on the couch. Janice's body language told him that Billy's breezy behavior had hurt her deeply. He resumed conversation, hoping to get her mind off what had just happened.

"Now that it's settled that we're going out, where would you like to go?" he asked.

Janice sighed, trying to hold back the tears. She must not let him see her cry. "I . . . I don't feel comfortable going out with you, Bill. Or should I call you *Buck* like everybody else?" Again she spat out his nickname.

"I really prefer Bill from you. That's the real me, you know." He smiled across the room. "I'm sorry you feel uncomfortable around me, Janice. I hope that changes. I really care about you."

"Look, I want some things understood right now," she said firmly.

"Sure," he said.

"First of all, I want it clear that you'd better not try to turn Billy's head. You live a wild life, and I've taught him better than that."

"Janice, I've explained to you that since I became a Christian I've changed. Maybe this doesn't make sense to you, but I just don't do what I used to do. You see, when Jesus Christ comes into your life, you get a brand-new set of desires and goals. I'm not looking for worldly things to make me happy anymore. I've found real, deep happiness with Jesus."

"Oh, yeah. That's why you're going to be in a movie. And what about your football career? Do you mean to tell me that doesn't mean anything to you any longer? Your whole life is money and fantasy. You have no idea what real life is like. Try crawling under a trailer when it's 50 below zero to tape the water pipes so they don't burst. Try raising a kid . . ." She stopped, then added, "You spout off about all this Christian stuff, but as far as I'm concerned it's all fantasy. You don't live in the real world!"

Bill wanted to tell her that Jesus Christ had made him see reality, but he was afraid that would lead nowhere. He knew he had to show her by his actions that he was different. Only God could work on her heart.

In the silence that followed, Janice pondered the problems involved in going out to dinner with her former husband. Her wardrobe consisted of two out-of-style dresses, several pairs of jeans, and some pullover shirts. She glanced at Bill's faded jeans. Maybe she would look okay. She decided she would go—only for Billy's sake, of course.

"Well, if I'm going anywhere, I'd better get ready," she said as she rose to leave the room.

"Great!" Bill stood politely.

"Oh, please," she said, rolling her eyes in irritation.

In her closet, she found a pink blouse she had forgotten she owned. She had bought it before Billy's accident, expecting to wear it to college. There had been no reason to wear it in the past two years, not even to the occasional school functions she attended with her son. She preferred to dress plainly at those times, in order to avoid unwanted attention from men who felt that her single status made her public property.

She gave the ruffled, western blouse a quick pressing and put it on with a fresh pair of jeans. Looking at herself in the mirror, she frowned. Gracie was right—she was too thin. She brushed her long hair and fluffed it around her face. *If I wore it to work like that,* she thought, *I'd get all kinds of attention.*

She pulled a small bag out of her dresser and took out the new mascara and blush she had bought the day before. With unsteady hands, she brushed the mascara on her long, blonde lashes. The effect pleased her. She gently applied the soft, pink blush to her cheeks. *Not bad,* she decided, lifting her chin in a glamorous pose.

When she came into the living room, Bill stood and whistled softly. "You look great in pink, Jan," he said. "And your hair . . . I like it down like that."

She wrinkled her nose at his compliment. In her room she had felt attractive enough. But after scanning his perfect tan, his perfect hair, his perfect everything, she was just a plain country waitress again.

When Billy returned from his chores, he needed a bath. While he hurried through that bothersome task, Janice and Bill found themselves once again sitting in the living room with nothing to say.

Finally Janice said, "You never did tell me how you found me."

"Your mother helped me."

"My mother!" Janice exclaimed, then whispered, "I thought she would be dead by now. How did she know where I was?"

"She didn't. She just had a copy of your Social Security card in the stuff you left. I traced you through that." Bill hoped she would ask some more questions.

"Mother," Janice said quietly, almost to herself, reflecting on a past she'd chosen to forget. "Is she still drinking? I'm surprised it hasn't killed her by now." Janice was shocked at her own callous words. Then again, what did she owe to the woman she had seldom seen sober?

Bill took a deep breath. He would enjoy telling this story.

"When you took off with Billy just after Pete died, her whole world collapsed. Oh, I know she was pretty bad off before that. But those two things almost put an end to her. She was found unconscious by a concerned neighbor who hadn't seen her for several days. That was about three months after you left."

Janice felt a stab of pain. She had been a "concerned neighbor" the previous winter when she found Old Man Lawson passed out drunk behind his trailer. Why couldn't she feel the same pity for her own mother?

Bill went on, "A woman from the community church down the street took her to the hospital, visited with her until she dried out, then took her into her own home. The church took up a collection and paid a lot of her bills, cleaned up the house, and got her a job. She, uh . . . she became a Christian soon after that."

Janice stared out the window behind Bill's head. "Hmm . . . Good for her . . . I hope it helped her stay sober."

"Yeah," Bill said, "it did. It helped her a lot. She became a different person." Seeing Billy come down the hall, he welcomed the distraction and said, "Hey, let's go eat!"

Billy had already laid out the plans for the evening. When Bill asked where they wanted to go, the boy named an expensive steakhouse twenty-five miles south of Pueblo, a place famous for its southwestern cuisine. Janice's protest was ignored, so the three climbed into the pickup truck and set out for dinner. Janice made sure Billy sat between her and Bill.

Despite the tension between Janice and Bill, conversation was not lacking. Billy replayed Sunday's football game for the entire ride and halfway into the meal.

At that point, Bill glanced at Janice, and she nodded in agreement.

"Billy," she began, "I . . . we have something to talk to you about."

Billy grinned. "Oh-oh. I guess I've been talking too much. Sorry." He began to devour his steak, looking expectantly at his mother.

Janice fumbled for words. "You know how we talked about . . . Well, we've dreamed that someday your leg . . . the way it didn't grow right after you broke it . . ." She looked at Bill for help.

"Billy, I've been talking to a doctor in Denver," Bill said. "He feels certain he can fix your leg so it will be as long as the other one. How would you like that?"

Billy swallowed hard and looked down self-consciously. After a moment he said, "What would he have to do?"

"I'm not exactly sure," Bill said. "But I do know it would mean an operation."

Billy glanced at his mother, then back at Bill. "Who would pay for it?" he asked.

"I would, Billy," Bill said.

Billy sat silently for a few minutes. "Why would you do that?"

Bill looked at Janice, who gave him a warning glare.

"Because I don't want the NFL to be deprived of a great future player," he said lightly.

Billy tried to smile.

Bill went on, "And because I think you're a great kid who deserves a chance. A lot of people helped me, Billy, with scholarships and things. I just want to pass it on."

Billy looked down at his plate for a long while. "Mom, what do you think?"

She laid her hand on his arm and squeezed. "It's up to you, Billy. You're almost grown up now. I've always loved you and been proud of you. I'll stand by you whatever you decide." She wanted him to reject Bill but not his gift. Unfortunately, the two came together.

"Would it hurt?" Billy asked Buck.

"Yeah, I think it would hurt a lot for a while," Bill said.

"But I could take it, couldn't I?" The boy looked at his hero hopefully.

"I'll be right there to make sure you can," Bill said.

Tears stung Janice's eyes. She felt like an outsider. Where had this instant superdad been through all the hundreds of boyhood hurts she had soothed away? And now suddenly he was the hero, and she was . . . She bit her lip to keep from speaking.

When the quiet trio returned to the trailer park that evening, Billy was deep in thought. His mom had taught him to work for things he wanted. And yet this chance to have his leg fixed so he could run normally and maybe play football after all was too good to turn down. And his mother was going to let him take it. That surely made it okay. It was like the things Mac and Gracie had done for them and the cowboy boots Buck had bought for him. But an operation was a lot more expensive. His mom was still paying for the medical care he'd had when he had the accident to begin with. Billy decided that life had become very exciting since Buck Mason had come into their lives, but it had also become very confusing.

"Come see my room, Buck," Billy said. He led Bill down the short hallway and into his room where pictures of the football hero papered the walls. Bill had to swallow hard and blink back tears when he noticed the movie ticket stub his son had saved from their first evening together.

After Billy went to bed, Bill confronted Janice again. "It would mean a lot if you would tell me you've forgiven me for the past."

"Why do you keep talking about forgiveness?" she said with unmistakable irritation in her voice. "The past is dead. Just do what you're going to do. I'm helpless now to stop you. If I lose Billy, at least I've done the right thing by letting you get his leg fixed."

"Lose Billy? But I'm not . . ."

"Just go, okay?" she interrupted, turning away from him.

Realizing it was useless to press the issue, he turned toward the door and then back again.

"I'll let you know the details as soon as I make Billy's appointment."

"Fine."

He heard the trembling in her voice and stepped closer. "Janice . . ."

Her back stiffened. "Good-bye," she growled.

"Good-bye," he whispered and disappeared out the door.

SIX

Bill had a heavy practice schedule the rest of the week. As the Mavericks' star quarterback, he was too important to the team to be away much. He knew Coach Speer was concerned about his players' preoccupation with other matters. A winning team requires a high level of concentration from every player. Consequently, personal problems had to be put aside during the season. Bill was a professional. His commitment to the game had earned him his place of honor and prestige.

But nothing had ever distracted him as much as his present concerns for Janice and Billy. He continued to wonder how ten years could have passed without his thinking more than a vague thought about them now and then. Each time he thought about that failure on his part, he asked the Lord for forgiveness.

One night during the week after he returned to Los Angeles, Bill sat in his spacious apartment trying to find an interesting television show to wind down from the day's practice. He pumped the remote control around the numerous stations available on cable. Nothing caught his eye, so he tossed the control onto the coffee table and wandered out onto his broad patio. The lights of the city below sparkled like stars but could not catch his eye.

His business manager had tried all week to make an appointment for Billy with the Denver doctor. But the doctor was in New York on a special case, and because the doctor was going to combine business with some vacation, his receptionist was uncertain exactly when he would return. If something didn't happen soon, Bill feared Janice would think he had been lying about wanting to help.

Bill tried calming his spirit by quoting Bible verses about trusting God and not being anxious. But peace of heart just wouldn't come. He tried praying, but his prayers didn't seem to rise above the ceiling.

Finally, in frustration he reached for the phone to call his pastor. Another disappointment. Dr. Miller was not in and was not expected until late. Bill began pacing the floor again.

After a while he sat down and dialed his teammate, Scott Lansing. Scott was one of the few people who knew about Bill's family situation and often prayed with him about it.

Bill chatted with Scott about the game coming up on Sunday, the weather, practice that day. Scott answered in monosyllables for a few minutes, then insightfully said, "What did you really call about, Buck? Do you need to talk?"

"Yeah," Bill answered, "I do." He paused, wondering where to start. "Man, I am so out of touch with God—I can't even pray right. Or maybe God just isn't listening."

"What makes you think that?" Scott asked.

"When I pray, I don't feel anything. No peace. Nothing."

"I see. Hey, Buck, where is that verse about how you can always depend on your feelings?" Scott said.

"Yeah, yeah, I know. But I feel like . . . I *know* I failed with Janice. When I think of all those years and how hard she's had to work just to take care of Billy . . . I was such a jerk. You should see the crummy trailer they live in. And she won't forgive me. I guess I don't deserve to be forgiven."

"Buck, when Jesus died, how many of your sins did He die for?"

"All of them, of course," Bill said, irritated by the question.

"Well, how many times does He need to forgive you for your past?"

Bill sighed. "I see your point. I know He's forgiven me, but—"

"Now you need to forgive yourself."

"That isn't easy when I think of all the wasted years," Bill said. "I feel rotten about everything I could have done but didn't."

"I know, Buck. But sometimes we have to overcome our feelings by choosing to think about what we know is right. Remember, 'forgetting those things which are behind.' Start thanking God for all your progress so far."

Bill was quiet for a moment as he considered his friend's words. He knew he could never go back and relive the past, and dwelling on his failures would just make him stumble.

"The Lord's gonna work it out, brother," Scott said. "He's gonna do what's best."

"Yeah," Bill said quietly.

"Do you believe it, Buck?"

"Yeah," Bill said, then laughed. "I have to *choose* to believe it, right?"

"Right!"

Practice went better for Bill the rest of the week. But even though he was again at his best, the Mavericks lost their game with the Los Angeles Raiders the following weekend. Nevertheless, the Mavericks had had a good season so far and had high hopes to make it to the Super Bowl in January. They were tied with Denver for the lead in their division and had already beaten that team once that season.

Despite the loss to the Raiders, things looked better to Bill the next Monday when he learned that his business manager had arranged Billy's appointment. He called Janice at the diner that morning to tell her it would be on a Wednesday two weeks later.

"I'll be there on Tuesday to pick both of you up," Bill told her. "We can stay at my favorite hotel in Denver that night and be fresh for the appointment."

Janice felt her heart leap with excitement at the prospect of her son's being made whole. It was an effort, but she gave a cool, brief answer. "We'll be ready."

"Maybe we can do some early Christmas shopping," Bill said.

Janice was quiet, so he continued, "Would that be all right with you?"

"Billy shouldn't miss any more school than necessary," she said.

"No, I suppose not. I can't miss too much practice either," Bill said. She was quiet again, so he went on, "Well, I'll see you in two weeks. Give my love to Billy."

"Your what?" she said.

"Sorry. Just tell him I said hello."

"Okay. Good-bye," Janice said, then dropped the receiver into its cradle.

Bill felt a surge of irritation. He prayed, "Lord, I know You have it under control. I know You're going to work it all out. Just please make Janice and Billy see that they need You, too."

Janice was ashamed of her rudeness. She tried to convince herself that this was the only way to protect Billy and to let Bill know she was watching his every move. Nevertheless, being unkind to Bill didn't give her any satisfaction.

Remembering how self-centered he had been in high school, she had to acknowledge that he had changed. But how could she admit that his changes made a difference to her? If she opened up to him, he might hurt her again. He might be playing up to her just so he could take Billy away.

Another thing nagged her. Always before, she and Billy had been close, sharing confidences with each other. But thanks to his great football hero, Billy had moved away from her emotionally. Now he wrote to Bill for advice. He didn't even associate with his school friends any more.

Janice knew the day would come when she would have to tell Billy the truth about his father. She had taught him to be truthful, but the time was coming when she would have to admit she'd been lying to him. What would that do to her son? What would it do to their relationship? She was trapped by her guilt and did not know how to shake herself free.

SEVEN

When the Mavericks played the Miami Dolphins on "Monday Night Football," they suffered their second defeat of the season. They could still reach the division playoffs if the Broncos lost to the Raiders, but they couldn't afford any more losses.

Billy watched the games intently. His mind seemed to take photograph after photograph as Buck executed play after play with amazing, consistent precision. Each time Buck was sacked by the huge defensive linemen of the opposing team, Billy groaned as if suffering the pain himself. He began to feel that he was one with Buck, and he dreamed of the day when he could actually play on a football team himself.

On the Saturday before Billy's appointment, Janice visited Mac and Gracie. As she entered their kitchen, she was alarmed by the tears on both of their faces.

"Hey, you two, what's up? What's wrong?" she said gently.

Mac looked at Gracie, and they both pointed to a letter on the kitchen table. Gracie dabbed at her tears as she said, "We never told you about our son Frankie."

"No," Janice said as she sat down and poured herself a cup of coffee. "I knew you had a son—I saw the pictures in your bedroom. But you didn't say anything about him, so I didn't want to ask. Kind of like me about Bill."

"Yeah," Mac said. "Some things are too painful to talk about. Just too much hurt."

"But this ain't a sad letter, kid." Gracie laughed and sobbed a little at the same time. "Our boy ain't dead or nothin'. In fact, he wants to come home. First time in eleven years we hear from him and he wants to come home. I tell you, I want to see that boy!"

"Would one of you please start from the beginning and tell me about it? It's only fair, you know," Janice said.

"Tell her, Ma," Mac answered.

"It's like this," Gracie said. "Frankie always had trouble in school. He got in with the wrong crowd, and they were doing drugs and booze. We never could figure out how they got it. We never knew he'd even do a fool thing like that. Guess we was pretty dumb. Anyway, to make a long story short, after a few brushes with the law, Frankie took off. He cleaned out the till, took all our savings—about two thousand dollars, and that was the last we heard of him until today.

"At first we was mad, then scared. After a while we knew we just wanted to see him again . . . Just to hear a word from him, to know he was okay. We could forgive him about the money." Gracie stopped her narrative long enough to wipe her eyes and blow her nose.

"This letter is from him," she said. "He's got his life straightened out. He's got a wife and . . . and a little baby." She began to sob into her handkerchief.

"We're grandparents," Mac said, shaking his head.

The three of them sat silently for a few minutes. Janice felt her heart reach out toward this loving couple who had been so good to her. She eyed the letter curiously, and Gracie shoved it across the table.

The letter was long and detailed. Neatly written in a feminine hand, it appeared that his wife had helped Frankie compose it. The letter began with Frankie asking his parents' forgiveness, followed by a full explanation of how he had spent the past eleven years. After leaving home, he had spent several years traveling with friends, supporting his drug habit by stealing.

Eventually the police had apprehended him, and he had been sentenced to five years in prison.

Prison had been a frightening experience for the young man. But he had been fortunate to meet some inmates who seemed different from the others. Frankie discovered that these men had had their lives changed by attending a Bible study. Drawn by what they had and he lacked, he joined their group. He said in his letter that he would tell his parents more about the Bible study and how he kicked drugs if they would let him come home. Janice knew what he would be telling them. It was like what happened to Bill.

Reading the letter stirred her memory. Hadn't she read in the Bible some story about a "prodigal" returning home? Were Frankie and Bill prodigals? What was the rest of the Bible story? She couldn't quite remember.

The letter went on to say that Frankie had been released early from prison. His parole officer was a Christian who made Frankie a part of his family. The reformed young man became active in church, where he met and married Alice. Now they had a six-month-old baby. With his parole completed and his slate wiped clean, Frankie wanted to come home and be reconciled with his parents. Would they let him come?

Janice brushed away tears as she finished the letter. "So what are you going to tell him?" she asked.

Mac sighed. "Well, for a long time I thought I'd die just to see him again. But now I don't know."

"Now, Mac," Gracie said in a soft voice so unlike her, "you know you could never turn the boy away. Especially not with a baby."

"No. No, I guess not." He studied the letter a moment. "That must be some little gal he's got there." He laughed. "Me a grandpa. Hey, Gramma." He lightly punched Gracie on the arm, and she slapped him back.

Janice looked on with great affection. She found herself looking forward to meeting Frankie and Alice Devine. And yet in a way she felt like she was on the outside. She dismissed the feeling immediately. Mac and Gracie had room in their hearts for everyone, not just their own flesh and blood. Still, it must be nice to have a complete family.

"Say, what's keeping us from calling him right now?" Gracie said. "Go ahead, call him, Pa."

Mac hesitated only a moment, then pulled the phone over from a side table. Carefully dialing the West Virginia number at the bottom of the letter, he waited as it rang. A soft click told the women that someone had answered, but Mac was silent, unable to speak.

"Hello . . . Hello." Frankie's faint voice could be heard. "Is someone there? Hello." He paused again, then said, "Pa? Is that you, Pa?"

Mac struggled to get his voice to work. Finally he choked out, "Frankie? Is that you, son?" Then he broke down in tears.

Gracie took the phone and spoke in a wavering voice. "Frankie, we love you. Come on home, baby. We want you to come home."

"I'll come home, Ma, as soon as I can. I gotta get some more money together, but we want to move out there. Is that okay?"

"Yeah, honey. But we can send you the money. Heck, your pa can come get you, can't you, Mac?" Gracie turned to Mac, who nodded. "Don't make us wait no longer. Come on home."

"We got a bunch of furniture to haul out there, Ma," Frankie explained.

"Listen, honey, we'll do whatever it takes," Gracie said.

Mac took the phone back. "Frankie . . . man, it's good to hear from you. Boy, I'll get a pickup and drive on out there. I'll leave tomorrow. We need to get you settled before the bad snow and ice cover the plains."

"That would be great. I can't wait to see you both. And, Pa . . ." Frankie stopped for a moment to regain control of his voice. "Pa, I love you. I'm gonna make up to you and Ma for all the grief I ever caused you. Just wait and see."

"Ain't no need, boy. Ain't no need," Mac mumbled into the phone. "Listen, give me your address and some directions. Tomorrow's Sunday. I figure I can be there by Tuesday afternoon . . . No . . . No, I'll drive carefully . . . Yeah, I'll stop at night." He wrote down directions on the back of Frankie's envelope. After a few more remarks and a good-bye from Gracie, they hung up.

The faces of the couple were shining with joy. Mac stared at the letter again and shook his head in disbelief. Then with a deep sigh he said, "Well, I guess I'd better get over to Browns' and see if Dave will loan me his pickup." Suddenly he realized his departure would create a problem. "Wait a minute . . . Janice, what about Billy's appointment? I can't leave Gracie to manage this place if you're gonna be gone Tuesday and Wednesday."

Janice had already come to a decision before he brought it up. She knew the diner was more than one person could handle, even with the younger waitresses to help. She also knew she would do nothing to waylay this chance for her friends' reunion with their son. They didn't dare wait another day with winter coming and the posssibility of snow threatening to make the trip hazardous.

"Bill can take Billy to Denver, Mac. It'll be okay," she said.

"Honey, are you sure?" Gracie laid her hand on Janice's and searched her face with concern.

"I'm sure," she said. "It was going to be awkward anyway. This lets me off the hook. You see, Billy hasn't been talking to me much about this. He seems to . . . well, to be drawing away from me. Maybe it's just time his . . . his father took over."

"You ain't told the boy yet, have you?" Mac asked.

"Oh, no," Janice sighed. "It has to be done soon, but I just don't know how. But listen, don't worry about us. I'm so happy for you both. This is the greatest! I guess our prodigals have both come back," she said.

"Our what?"

"Oh, nothing. Just a story I read somewhere. I'm going to go tell Billy the news." She rose and walked to the door. "And listen, you guys, I'm glad for you . . . Really glad."

Back in her trailer, Janice picked up the Bible she now kept on the coffee table. She began thumbing through a listing of key words in the back. She looked for "prodigal" but couldn't find it. Next she tried "sons" and found a passage that looked familiar—Luke, chapter 15, verses 11 through 32. She looked in the front of the Bible for the page number of Luke and was soon reading the story titled "The Prodigal Son."

As Janice read the story, she saw how it compared with what had happened to Mac and Gracie's son. The Bible story told of a man whose son had gone to a distant land and wasted his money on partying and immoral living. When he saw the result of his sinful ways, he went back home to his father, who freely forgave him in spite of all the pain the son had caused him.

Janice began reading the story again, this time with herself in mind, thinking about how Bill had wronged her and had come back for forgiveness after all this time. But somehow the Bible tale didn't fit her situation. She had shut Bill out. Soon the thought began to creep into her mind that she had been more like the wandering son, considering the way she had deserted her own mother. Viewing the situation from Mac and Gracie's perspective made her think of what her mother must have gone through all those years. She had lost her husband by desertion and her son by tragic accident. Then Janice had taken Billy and left without a trace. Janice recalled with remorse what Bill had said about her mother's collapse. Now a mom herself, she understood the pain her leaving had caused her mother.

It also occurred to Janice that Bill could have told her mother at any time where to find her, once he'd located her in the southern Colorado community. Apparently he hadn't. Or maybe he had, and her mother was waiting for Janice to make the first move.

If there had been any chance her mother was still a drunk, Janice wouldn't have bothered to think about her again. She would not take Billy to a drunk old woman and say, "This is your grandmother." But somehow she knew that just as Bill and Frankie had changed when they became Christians, so had her mother. What was she like now? Janice closed her eyes and tried to envision her old home in Alabama. It was a dismal picture.

Janice felt a deep ache in her chest, and no matter how hard she tried, she couldn't make it go away. Tears began to flow down her cheeks, and she covered her face and sobbed.

Billy came out of his room to show his mother a picture of Buck Mason he'd found in a new magazine. Seeing her crying, he hurried to sit beside her on the couch.

"Mom, what's the matter?"

Janice quickly composed herself. "Oh, Billy, these are happy tears," she lied. She told him the story of Mac and Gracie's son.

"That's neat, Mom!" Billy said when she told him Mac would be bringing the young family home by the end of the week. "Mac and Gracie deserve the best!"

Janice smiled at her son. "Do you know what this means?"

"No. What?"

"It means I have to stay and help Gracie at the diner this week. You'll have to go with Buck alone to Denver for your appointment."

"Oh, that's no problem," he said. "It'll be great, in fact. No women to get in the way." Then he added sheepishly, "No offense, Mom. But you know how it is, don't you?"

Janice looked down and said, "Get me a hankie, honey. All these tears have made a mess of my face."

Billy really *was* moving away from her. Her world was falling apart. But for his sake, she would maintain some semblance of calm assurance that all would be well. All these years she had been what he needed; she would not stop now.

As Billy handed her a tissue, she smiled. "You and Buck will have a great time. Denver is a fun place to visit."

"I can't wait to stay in a fancy hotel. Buck says we're going to the Majestic Inn out by the airport. I wonder if it's like the snooty places they show on TV," he mused. Then he remembered the magazine. "Hey, look, Mom. Here's a picture of Buck in my new magazine. Read what it says."

Janice took the book and saw Bill's handsome face staring out at her. The caption read, "Where is football's most handsome quarterback running off to between games these days? Is some Colorado cowgirl about to lasso this very eligible bachelor?" Her eyes widened. This was too much.

"Oh, Billy, why do you read such garbage? Get rid of that thing!" She shoved the magazine back at him. To change the subject before he could say more, she said, "Go fix us each a peanut butter sandwich, okay?"

"Sure, Mom," Billy said. But he grinned to himself as he went to obey. Was his own mother that "Colorado cowgirl"? She seemed too old for his pal Buck, but maybe Buck would overlook that. The possibilities sure provided interesting food for thought.

EIGHT

Mac borrowed a pickup truck from a rancher friend and left early Sunday morning for West Virginia. To those he left behind, the next few days would seem an eternity. For Gracie, there was the anticipation of seeing her son after so many years and of meeting his wife and baby. For Janice and Billy, there was the trial of waiting to see Bill and finding out what could be done for Billy's leg. For all of them, the time dragged ever so slowly.

On Monday Janice called the school and arranged for Billy's absence. Billy was a good student, and one teacher volunteered to come to the trailer after his surgery to help him keep up with his class.

Bill arrived on Tuesday, coming to the Pueblo airport and renting a comfortable family car. As he drove toward the trailer court south of town, he tried to calm the butterflies in his stomach. He asked the Lord to give him peace and to help him say the right things to Janice. She had been so cold to him on the phone! Yet, he was confident that someday all his prayers and those of his friends would reach through her bitterness and Janice would know the freedom she could have in forgiving him. His part in bringing her to that point was to stay close to the Lord and not let his emotions demand an immediate resolution of the conflict. He would wait to see how she felt today before trying to engage in any meaningful conversation.

That morning Janice had cooked for the breakfast shift at

the diner, and then Gracie took over. Janice went home to get Billy ready, planning to go back for the evening shift.

Billy hurried around without accomplishing a thing while Janice packed his backpack.

"Calm down, honey," she said.

"Okay, Mom," he said. But he couldn't. So he paced the living room for over an hour before Bill finally pulled into the driveway. He bounded out the door to greet him, backpack in hand.

"I'm ready! Let's go," he shouted as he came out.

"Hang on, buddy," Bill said with a laugh as he stepped out of the car. "Where's your mom? Is she ready yet?"

Just as Janice came to the door, Billy was happily telling Bill, "She can't go. She has to stay and work at the diner."

Bill frowned at her in dismay. "What's going on, Janice?"

"Come in a minute," she said. She tried to avoid his gaze, but his eyes kept searching hers as though he were trying to see into her soul. She looked at the floor and out the window—*anywhere* her eyes could wander as she explained why Mac had to leave town and why she had to stay home to work in the diner. Finally she turned and went into the kitchen.

"You two have fun. I'll see you tomorrow night," she said. "I put Billy's medical records in his backpack."

Bill shook his head. "I'm sorry you can't make the trip, Jan. Look, Billy can call you tonight after we're settled in at the hotel. Okay?"

"Okay," she answered. "I'll be at the diner."

"I'm really sorry you're not coming with us."

She was silent for a moment, struggling to find words to tell him something—or perhaps to ask him a question. She wanted to talk to him about the aching in her heart over her mother— the pain that wouldn't go away. Maybe he would have an answer for her. But after she'd treated him so rudely, would he even care about her anymore?

Sensing she wanted to say more, Bill waited, hoping this

might be the opening he had prayed for. Meanwhile, Billy had settled himself in the front seat of the car and was honking the horn every two or three minutes. But Bill couldn't leave now— not if Janice wanted to talk. As she turned slowly back to him, he saw the struggle in her face and stepped closer to her, reaching out his hand to take hers, his eyes full of understanding. But she put her hand up to stop him and shook her head.

"Not now. When you come back, we'll talk," she said.

"I'd like that."

She nodded. Billy set off the car horn again, this time long and loud. Janice smiled at her son's youthful impatience.

"You'd better go," she said.

Bill's smile was so dazzling, her heart seemed to leap within her. Suddenly everything looked brighter.

"Good-bye," she said, looking toward the door.

"Bye, Janice. I'll take good care of Billy."

"I know you will," she replied as he went out the door.

"It's going to work out all right," she assured herself as she watched the sedan drive away.

Bill and Billy chatted enthusiastically as they drove through Pueblo and north toward Colorado Springs. Interstate 25 gave the travelers a breathtaking view of the mountains as well as short travel time between Colorado's three largest cities. The highway passed majestic Pike's Peak and the United States Air Force Academy, where training planes made constant touch-and-go landings.

Bill decided to make use of his time alone with Billy, hoping to find out how much the boy understood about God. Bill had written several letters to his son explaining his own beliefs. He had sent a pocket New Testament along with one letter, having marked some verses to read. He thought often these days of all the wasted years in Billy's life, when so many wrong ideas could have been put into the boy's mind. Now he was determined to overcome any of his son's misconceptions about his Creator.

Asked whether he thought God was the Maker of our universe, the youngster responded, "Sure, I believe God created the world. I think it took Him a long time though . . . millions of years. One of my teachers said God got it all started, then sat back to see what would come of it. Another teacher taught us about evolution and kind of made fun of people who believe in God. But I don't go along with that. See, if there isn't a God, there isn't a heaven. And my dad is in heaven. I really believe that." Billy looked at Bill for a look of agreement or affirmation.

Bill nodded, unable to speak. When Billy learned the truth about their relationship, how would that affect his thoughts about God? Would he feel he'd been lied to about his earthly father and maybe about his heavenly Father too? Bill hated keeping the secret any longer, but he knew that for now he had to.

"Hey, you guys are gonna win the AFC championship. I can just feel it!" Billy said, changing the subject. "You're gonna win the Super Bowl too!"

"We're planning on it, pal. We almost made it last year, remember?"

"Yeah. Miami got you in the last quarter in a playoff game. Man, I was really disappointed," Billy said. "How did it feel to lose when you were so close?"

"I take it a lot better now than I did two years ago. When I became a Christian, it changed my outlook on just about everything, including football. I still want to be the best in the National Football League, but God's higher purpose for my life puts winning and losing in perspective." Bill was proud of himself for getting the conversation back to the Lord.

"What does 'higher purpose' mean?" Billy asked, wrinkling his brow. "I think football is a pretty high purpose itself. Especially when the Mavericks are winning." He grinned at Bill.

Bill smiled back but continued his train of thought. "God created me, so my life belongs to Him. It's my purpose in life to tell people how much He loves them and how He has provided a way for them to spend eternity with Him in heaven. You see, Billy, long after I finish playing football I can still tell people about God's love. In fact, football is third on my list of what's really important."

"What's first and second?"

"God is first and, uh . . ." Bill realized he had almost said too much. "Family is second," he finished vaguely.

"Oh," Billy said, trying to recall what he had read about Buck's family. Since he couldn't remember anything, he was quiet, not wanting to appear uninformed. He'd thought he knew everything about Buck.

It bothered Bill that he couldn't stir up curiosity in Billy about the Lord. The boy always passed over his comments and quickly went on to other subjects. Bill wondered how he could make his son see that he needed to be saved.

They arrived at their destination in the late afternoon and continued on the interstate highway through most of Denver. Billy's eyes were wide with wonder as he saw the size of the city. He pointed out various interesting sights and pumped Bill for information about all of them.

Bill found the turnoff to Interstate 70 and turned east, then took the exit that led to the boulevard where the Majestic Inn stood tall and proud.

Billy stared at the impressive building. The entire front of the four-story lobby was made of glass, and the brilliant chandeliers made it sparkle like diamonds. Bill smiled at Billy's awestruck expression.

The doorman opened the car door for Billy, and the valet took Bill's place behind the wheel. A uniformed bellhop came to get their luggage. He looked somewhat askance at Billy's shabby backpack, but the boy was too engrossed in the sights of the hotel to notice. Bill led his son through the great glass door held by the doorman. They approached the large front desk, where the clerk recognized the famous football star.

"Ah, yes, Mr. Mason. Welcome to Denver. We have your rooms ready. We have given you the suite on the tenth floor. It has an excellent view of the Colorado Rockies from the balcony. As requested, we also have reserved a single room down the hall with a similar view. The roses you ordered are in the suite, and the fruit as well." The efficient man turned the register toward Bill and handed him a pen.

"There's been a change," Bill said as he signed. "We won't be needing the single room."

"Very well, sir. Here is your key." The clerk presented it to the bellhop, who preceded the two to the elevator.

Billy's experience in elevators had been limited to going up one floor in a Pueblo shopping mall. As he felt the hotel elevator moving upward, his stomach seemed to rise into his throat.

Bill chuckled at his son's wide-eyed expression.

They got off on the tenth floor. The bellhop led the way to their room, unlocking the door and letting them enter first. The ceremony and service, as well as the luxury of the suite, amazed Billy. A large basket of fruit sat on the coffee table in front of a plush, velvet couch. Billy stared at the arrangement. Among the apples, oranges, and pears were tiny pewter football figures wired onto sticks.

"Is this for me?" he asked.

"That's for you," Bill answered, enjoying the happy light in his son's eyes.

"Gee, thanks, Buck," the boy said. He took a shiny apple to eat. The heavy pewter figures felt expensive. He carefully removed them from their sticks and began playing with them on the table.

Bill took the newspaper provided by the hotel and searched for some evening entertainment.

NINE

Living in a rural area where physical prowess was more important than appearance, Billy had never really studied his own face in a mirror. Dirty marks, uncombed hair, and unbrushed teeth all passed his hurried inspection as he moved on to the more important things in life—like football, TV, or playing around with the guys. But now as he observed his hero, he wanted to copy everything the man did.

First, he tried to copy Buck's unique walk, but his limp prevented that. He settled for improving his posture and swinging his shoulders like Buck did, and also using aggressive hand gestures when he talked. Then he noticed Buck was always well-groomed and even smelled good. His mom had kept him as clean as possible, but lately he had put off her attempts at grooming him. He had, however, taken the hint when she'd put a deodorant stick on his pillow last summer.

As Billy waited for his new friend to take him out to dinner, he became bored and decided to watch as Bill stood at the bathroom mirror combing his hair.

Bill had made a commercial for men's hair products because his own unique look had become popular. While some men spent a lot of money to achieve the stylish wave, Bill simply took advantage of mousse, a blow-dryer, and a natural cowlick.

Billy watched from the doorway as Bill smoothed his hair into place. His own hair was shaggy and unstyled. He marveled at the products Bill lined up on the bathroom counter just for grooming.

Bill glanced at him in the mirror, amused at the expression on the boy's face. "Want to try some?" he offered.

Billy grinned. "Naw." Then, "Can you show me how you comb your hair?"

"Sure." Bill handed him a comb. "Take this and start about here. Then give it a flip, like this." He demonstrated with his own hair.

Billy tried. "Like this?" It was an awkward try, but the result promised better things to come.

"Try again," Bill said. "Here . . ." He sprayed some styling mousse on his hand and pushed it through Billy's hair. A quick blast of the blow-dryer and an expertly turned comb brought about a transformation.

"Pretty sharp," Bill said.

"Pretty sharp," Billy echoed. Then he looked at Bill and back at himself in the mirror with a pleased smile, as if seeing himself for the first time. Suddenly a trace of a frown crossed his brow. He shook his head slightly as if to erase what he was seeing. He looked at Bill, who was still grooming himself, and confusion crept into the boy's face. He turned to leave the bathroom, then turned back as if he were hoping to make a lie of what he'd just seen.

His face was Buck's face, only younger! Their faces were the same! From the ice-blue eyes and black, wavy hair and cowlick, to the chin line and the slight dimple at the right corner of their mouths, they were alike. Two people could not look more the same unless they were twins, and their ages prevented that. That left only one possibility. But how could that be?

Billy went into the bedroom and sat on the edge of the bed, grabbing a pillow and clutching it fiercely. He stared at the floor, shaking his head. Now the stares and the veiled whispers of the kids at school finally began to make sense. All of them had seen the resemblance. Man, was he ever stupid!

Bill watched his odd behavior and followed him into the bedroom. "Billy? What's the matter, pal?"

"I wanna talk to my mom," Billy answered through clenched teeth.

Baffled, Bill picked up the phone and put through the call to the diner. As the phone began to ring, he handed it to Billy.

The boy took it, listened for a moment, then said, "Gracie, let me talk to my mom."

At the diner, Janice called another waitress over to the grill, where hamburgers sizzled next to some steaks. "I have a call from Billy," she said. Wiping her hands on her apron, she took the phone. "Hi, honey. How are you doing?"

"Mom . . . Mom . . . who is . . . who *was* Pete Griffin?"

Janice gasped. Bill had broken his promise! She took a deep breath, blinked back the tears that were involuntarily forming, and struggled for the right words.

"Mom, who was Pete Griffin?" Billy raised his voice only a little.

"Billy . . . Pete Griffin was my big brother," she said slowly.

"Then . . . who is Buck Mason?" he asked.

"Bill Mason is . . . he's your father." The last two words were almost a whisper, but Billy knew what she had said.

"Then I'm illegit . . . illegit . . ." He could not bring himself to pronounce the word.

Unmindful of the sudden quiet in the diner, Janice cried, "No! No, Billy, you're not illegitimate. We were married. Honest, honey. We got divorced, that's all. Lots of people get divorced."

She waited a moment for his answer, but he was silent.

"Billy? Billy, I love you," she said. He didn't answer. "Billy, let me talk to Buck."

Billy shoved the phone receiver at Bill without looking at him, then stood and walked into the living room.

"Janice?" Bill had watched with complete bewilderment at what had happened.

"Why did you tell him?" she shouted.

"Janice, I promise, I didn't tell him anything. He just suddenly got real upset and wanted to call you. I don't know what happened!"

She was quiet for a moment. "I'm coming up there. Tell Billy I'll be there in three hours."

Janice hung up and turned around. The patrons in the small diner quickly looked down at their meals and began to talk quietly. Janice turned to Gracie, who had come over to the phone. "Gracie, I have to go. Billy knows."

"Go, girl," the older woman urged. "We'll manage. You just take care of yourself and your family."

Janice faced the dining room again. "Did I hear somebody say they're going to Denver tonight?"

"Yo!" Old George called across the room.

Janice came to his table. "George, can I hitch a ride with you? My boy . . ."

"Say no more, missy. I'll get you there," he said gently. "We can go right now."

Janice threw off her apron and grabbed her jacket. George took a last hurried bite. Gracie refused his payment for the meal, so the two went out to the eighteen-wheeler full of bawling cattle bound for the Denver stockyards. As Janice climbed in, she was aware of the smell of the cattle and remembered her own need of a bath. After a day of cooking in the diner, her hair drooped and grease spots decorated her shirt. But nothing mattered right then except Billy, her son whom she should have told the truth so long ago.

For quite some time after they drove away from the diner, both George and Janice were quiet. The plaintive strains of a country song came softly over the radio. Janice stared out the window, not seeing the brilliant sunset over the western mountains. As they drove through Pueblo and headed toward Colorado Springs, she thought about Billy and how she had never been away from him before. Even after his accident, she had slept in the hospital waiting room and checked on him often. Now he was so far away and needed her so much.

She agonized over not telling him sooner that Bill was his father. If she had done that, maybe he would have accepted it more easily and with less distress. Her bitterness against Bill, her desire to punish him for the years of hardship and loneliness, had led her to keep silent. And now Billy was the one being punished, the one being hurt the most. Over and over in her mind she examined her life, and the harder she looked, the more flaws she saw. She had not even cared if her own mother lived or died. She had drawn a little circle around herself and Billy, only letting in those people who she was sure would never hurt them.

As she began to see how wrong her motives had been, tears came to her eyes. She unconsciously reached out and touched a large sticker pasted on the dashboard. "Need a friend? Try Jesus," it read. As her eyes focused on it, George spoke.

"Yup, Jesus is the One all right. Help for any problem."

Surprised at his comment, Janice stared at the wrinkled, old man in the dim light of the cab. George always chewed tobacco and wore the same type of plaid shirt and dusty jeans. Despite his rough clothes, his manners made him the kind of customer Janice liked most. He treated her with respectful friendliness and always had a good word for everyone; his gentle eyes were surrounded with leathery smile lines.

George glanced at her, spat tobacco into a can by the door, then studied the road in front of him.

"Worried about your boy." It was more of a statement than a question. "His daddy'll take care of him."

"How long have you known?"

"Take a blind fool not to see. I ain't the only one who know'd it."

"But no one ever said anything."

"Weren't no need," he drawled.

Janice felt a warm glow of gratitude for George and the other unknown friends who had seen Billy's remarkable resemblance to Bill but kept it to themselves. "You're really something, George. Thanks."

"'Tain't me. It's Him." He nodded toward the bumper sticker.

Once again Janice reached out and touched it. Her finger rested on the word "Jesus." Alone in her thoughts again, she wondered if God could really help. Then the panic about Billy returned. It frightened her to think of him struggling to sort out her lies.

O God, she thought, *please help me. Please, please help me. If You'll just hold on to Billy, make him be okay, don't let him do anything foolish, I'll . . . I'll really try to understand what You're all about. Jesus, if You really are God, help me.*

She sat back and sighed. Gradually a deep calm came over her, as though God had touched her heart. That was a new thought for her, but she felt it was true. This was not her old bravado of "everything will turn out somehow," but rather a warmth that came both from within and without and filled her with the assurance that God would indeed make things work out right. A peaceful look came over her face, and George, seeing it in the dim light of the truck cab, smiled to himself.

As soon as Bill hung up the phone, he called out to Billy. There was no answer, so he went into the living room of the hotel suite. Billy was not there. Concern filled Bill's mind as he checked the bathroom, the balcony, and even the closets, gradually realizing that the boy had fled. Racing out the door, quickly checking both ways up and down the hall, he started toward the stairway, then turned back to the elevator.

Lord, help me find Billy. Keep him out of trouble, he prayed. He asked himself how this could have happened, and as if the Lord spoke to him directly, he knew the answer. While the two of them had stood before the mirror, he had again been reminded of their look-alike faces. But Billy must have seen it for the first time. Bill could picture the way Billy had shaken his head in disbelief, and he realized the boy had grasped the truth at that very moment.

As Bill searched the lobby and several of the shops, he asked himself why he had not talked Janice out of such a foolish charade. It was amazing that their son had not noticed the resemblance before. For the boy to spend all his life thinking his father was a dead hero, then suddenly to come face to face with the living father who had abandoned him—it had obviously been too much to take. And the fact that his father was wealthy and famous while he and his mother lived near poverty . . . what kind of father would . . . Bill could only imagine what the boy must be thinking. All he could see was the anguished expression on his son's face and the fact that he had run away from his newfound father.

Bill went to the hotel clerk and inquired if he had seen Billy. The man said no but promised to notify Bill if he saw him. Bill debated whether or not to call the police. Should he risk the publicity that might bring? Deciding against it, he went out the front door of the hotel and tried to figure out where an angry twelve-year-old might go. How far could he go on that bad leg?

Bill looked back and forth in all directions and finally decided to walk toward the residential area east of the hotel. Feelings of frustration consumed him as he walked, then ran, then walked again. One moment he prayed and felt God's presence with him. The next moment he recalled the look on Billy's face, and panic rose again.

Darkness crept over Denver as the sunset faded behind the snow-covered mountains. Streetlights began to glow and brighten in the dark. Bill began to realize that one person alone would never be able to find the boy. He began to feel the cold of the November night, and he remembered that Billy would not have taken his coat. Bill walked the long blocks back to the hotel, wishing he had had the presence of mind to search for Billy in his car.

Once he had retrieved his own coat and Billy's from their room, he had his car brought by the hotel valet and drove in a different direction to continue his search. The worried father was frightened—it all seemed so hopeless.

TEN

George and Janice began their hundred-mile journey a few miles south of Pueblo at the diner and took the interstate bypass through Colorado Springs. George nursed his giant eighteen-wheeler up and over long hills, then faced dangerous downslopes and curves that took all of his considerable experience to navigate as the heavy truck gained momentum. All the time the cattle were bawling in the wind, as if they knew they were bound for the Denver stockyards and eventually someone's dinner table.

Janice thought the trip would never end, but they finally came over the last hill where the lights of Denver stretched before them from halfway up the mountains and far out onto the eastern Colorado plains. It was a breathtaking sight George never failed to appreciate for its beauty and for the fact that his journey was almost over. For Janice, the latter reason was sufficient.

George ignored the "No Trucks" signs posted along the street leading to the Majestic Inn. Pulling up in front of the elegant establishment, he stuffed several dollars in Janice's jacket pocket, patted her hand, and said, "I'll be praying for you, missy."

She smiled a weary smile. "I guess I was pretty dumb to forget my purse. I don't even have tip money in my pocket for a phone call. Thanks, George. I'll pay you back."

She jumped out of the truck. "I hope you don't get a ticket," she called as he drove away.

The front desk clerk of the hotel stared out the window with disgust. He saw the illegal truck, the transfer of money, and the disreputable young woman disembarking. To his horror, she ran past the doorman, into the Inn, and right up to his desk.

"Please," she said, "I need to know Buck Mason's room number."

"My dear young, eh, *lady*," the clerk said disdainfully, "we are not in the custom of giving out our guests' room numbers to every passing . . ."

"But I have to see Mr. Mason," she said.

"Madam, many women want to see Buck Mason. I'm sorry—I must ask you to leave."

"Janice!" Bill had just returned from his unfruitful search. Seeing Janice at the front desk, he quickly came to her aid.

To the amazement of the desk clerk, the famous football player approached the dingy, little creature and embraced her. *What on earth* . . . The two then hurried out the front door, leaving the pompous man to watch their exit with mouth agape.

As they settled in the car, Bill explained that Billy had run away and that he had been searching worriedly for him for three hours.

"Where have you looked?" Janice asked.

"All around the neighborhood, for blocks in each direction," Bill said as he drove down the avenue. "He could be hiding anywhere."

"Why didn't you try the shopping mall back that way?" she asked, pointing in the opposite direction of their travel. "That's the obvious place for a kid to go."

Bill felt the rebuke. He had no idea where a twelve-year-old boy, even his own twelve-year-old son, would go when he was upset. Bill turned the car around at the next opening in the median strip and raced the mile and a half to the mall. He had not even noticed the place on his way to the hotel.

The parking lot was nearly full. Bill found a parking space only after driving around for several minutes. As they got out of the car, Janice took Billy's coat. She held it close, thinking of the boy who should be wearing it.

Bill came around the car and pulled her gently into his arms.

"Would it be okay with you if we pray before we look?" he asked, looking into her upturned face.

Janice pulled back. It had been a relief for Bill to give her a quick hug in the hotel after the rude treatment by the desk clerk. But this time she moved away from him. Nevertheless, she nodded in agreement to his suggestion.

"Father, we need Your help. You know where Billy is. Please take care of him, and lead us to him quickly," Bill prayed.

They went into the mall and found a directory. Janice scanned the listing.

"Let's see . . . Sporting goods stores. Computer centers. Let's try those," she said. She turned and marched through the crowds of shoppers with Bill following. The muscular football player wasn't used to following along like a meek little lamb, but he didn't know what else to do.

After fruitless searches in two stores, they spotted Billy leaning against the front window of a sporting goods store and staring at a copy of the same poster of Buck Mason that adorned his bedroom wall. His bitter expression was reflected in the glass.

Janice and Bill pushed through the crowds toward him. Then Bill stopped and held Janice back.

"Janice, let me talk to him first. Please?"

Tears filled her eyes. She reluctantly nodded her assent.

Bill approached his son and stood several feet away, looking at the poster. It was a remarkable photograph. His determined expression had been clear as the football was leaving his hand. It had been a game-winning play. Then Bill saw the face of his son, so like his own and so deeply troubled. He started to speak, but Billy shot him an angry glare.

"You were there all the time. You were out there playing football while my mom was working so hard." Billy paused, his jaw clenched. "She's too good for you, Buck Mason!" He spat the name out just as Janice had done. "You didn't care about us! You can go back to where you came from and never come back!"

Billy whirled around and limped toward Janice, not giving Bill a chance to respond. He allowed her to hold him close and put his coat around his shoulders.

"Mom, we don't need him. And we aren't going to accept anything he wants to give us. Nothing! I'll take care of you."

Janice looked up into Billy's face and brushed back his shaggy hair. How he had grown recently! "Oh, Billy, what can I say?"

"I'm almost grown up. Pretty soon I'll be able to drive, and I'll drive a truck . . ."

"Billy, we have so many things to explain to you," Janice said. She looked toward Bill for help.

"We don't need him!" Billy shouted.

Before Janice could say more, Bill found himself accosted by a group of teenagers.

"Wow, it's Buck Mason! Hey, can we have your autograph? Hey, look everybody—Buck Mason is here!"

Crowds began to surround Bill, separating him from Janice. He tried to graciously decline their requests but found himself signing his name to numerous pieces of paper.

"Let them have the bum," Billy said, pulling Janice away.

Janice glanced toward Bill. Was this what happened every time he went anywhere? What an awful life he must have! She hesitated, then went with Billy. They would wait for Bill in the car.

Out in the cold November night, Janice put her arm around Billy and guided him to where they had parked the car.

"I don't want to get in. We can walk," he said.

"Walk where, honey? To Pueblo?"

"Call Gracie."

"She can't leave the diner, and she doesn't have a car anyway."

"Can't we go someplace else?" Billy's eyes scanned the parking lot for an escape route.

"Oh, Billy, let's just go back to the hotel with Bill. After the three of us talk, we'll decide what to do," Janice stated calmly.

After a quarter of an hour, they saw Bill running toward the car. He jumped in and started the motor, waving and smiling to the young people who had followed him.

Billy slumped in the backseat in disgust.

The three rode back to the hotel in silence. Ignoring the looks of the desk clerk, Bill guided Janice and Billy to the elevator. Once they were in the suite, he phoned room service and ordered dinner.

Billy slumped on the couch, refusing to talk or eat. When Janice could not coax him to even taste anything, she told him to go to bed.

"You'll feel better in the morning," she told him. She sat on his bed and rubbed his back just like she used to when he was small. Gradually his tight muscles relaxed.

"Billy?" Janice said.

"Mmmm?" he murmured.

"It's not like it was all Buck's—I mean, your father's—fault."

"Don't call him that!" His muscles tensed again.

"Shhh. Okay. Just relax." She waited a moment. "We both made a lot of mistakes."

"Not you!"

"Yes, me. Both of us were very young when you were born. When we got divorced, I made it very hard for us to be found by using my maiden name. You know, Billy . . . I lied to you, telling you my poor, dead brother was your father. That was wrong. And . . . and I never have told you about my mother."

"Your mother?"

"Yes. You have a grandmother. Buck told me she's still living in the same house I grew up in. How about that?" She paused. "It really broke her heart when I took you and ran away."

Billy turned over, suddenly curious. "Why did you leave?"

"Oh, there were too many problems I didn't want to own up to. I was just too young to handle them. I wanted to run away with you and start over someplace new."

He blinked his eyes, yawning. "I won't run away from you, Mom. I'll take care of you."

"I love you, Billy." She touched his cheek, and he smiled, his eyes closing involuntarily.

"I love you too, Mom."

Soon his even breathing told Janice he was asleep, and she rose from his bed, realizing how tired she was from the long workday and the emotional struggles of the evening.

When she emerged from the bedroom, she closed the door and rested against it for a moment. Bill came over and pulled her gently into his arms. This time she did not resist. It felt good to rest her head against his broad chest. She had forgotten how tall he was. The top of her head was even with his shoulders.

"Oh!" She pulled back and laughed with embarrassment. "Don't touch me. I'm a mess!"

"I hadn't noticed," he said, taking her hand and leading her to the couch. "Hmm . . . is that egg yolk on your shirt?"

"Egg yolk, hamburger grease, gravy . . . you name it, I can cook it."

He pulled her down on the couch beside him. She moved away several inches but still let him hold her hand.

"Janice . . . I love you," he said.

"You're crazy, you know that?" She pulled her hand away but without irritation.

"No, I'm not crazy. You're steady and reliable and smart— everything I'm not."

"You've done pretty well for yourself. That was a three million dollar contract you signed this year, I believe. Or was it four?"

"That's just luck. Do you know how many high school and

college athletes train all their lives for the pros, then never make it? Besides, in other ways I've been a loser."

She laughed. "Oh, yeah . . . I'm sure."

"I robbed you of a lot when I got you pregnant," he said. "You were a good student. You could have accomplished so much."

She looked at him in surprise. "I have Billy."

Her response startled him. Despite all it had cost her, she had made their son the focus of her life, heaping on him the love Bill had rejected. Unlike him, she had always understood what was most important in life: people—family. That made Bill love her all the more.

After a few moments he said, "Did you talk to Billy?"

"Some. But he was pretty tired. We'll talk some more in the morning."

"Do you think he'll go to the doctor with us?"

"I think I can talk him into it," she said, but secretly she wondered if she could.

They were quiet again for a few minutes. Bill wanted to ask her why she was so different this time, why she seemed to be opening up. But he was afraid to break the spell. When she looked up at him, he was tempted to kiss her, but he knew it was a bad idea. He had risked taking her into his arms because she looked so small and vulnerable, and because he loved her so much. He wanted her to feel safe and secure with him. He wanted to regain the trust he had callously thrown away years ago.

"Have you talked to my mother since that time you saw her?" she asked.

"Yeah. I called her after the first time I saw you and Billy."

Janice nodded but said nothing more. She had been up since 4 that morning, and her body ached with fatigue. She laid her head against the back of the couch and sighed. The plush velvet seemed to enfold her, and she felt as though she were floating.

Soon her even breathing told Bill she was asleep. He gently laid her head against a throw pillow, removed her shoes, and pulled her legs onto the couch. He found a spare blanket in the bedroom and covered her, then gathered a few of his things and quietly left the suite.

ELEVEN

Early the next morning, Janice awoke with a start as sunlight began to reflect off the snow-covered mountains through the balcony doors. For a moment she struggled to remember where she was. Then the events of the previous day exploded in her mind, and she jumped up and ran to the bedroom. Billy lay sleeping soundly where she had left him the night before. She sighed with relief at the sight of her son. Bill was not anywhere in the suite.

She felt clammy from sleeping in her clothes. She looked in Billy's backpack and took out his extra shirt. Fortunately, it was one she had bought for him to "grow into," so it fit her as well. Her jeans would have to do, but at least she would have a clean shirt on. She showered and washed her hair, then enjoyed using the hair-dryer provided by the hotel.

Billy had not yet awakened. The clock on the bedside table read 9:30. His appointment was for 11:30. She decided to let him sleep for a few more minutes.

The sound of the door being unlocked in the living room startled her, but she was relieved to see it was Bill carrying an armload of packages.

"Good morning, beautiful," he said as he unloaded the packages onto the couch.

"Hi."

"I bought you some things since I saw you didn't have time to pack before you left home," he said.

She frowned, but curiosity got the better of her. Bill took her by the hand and sat her on a chair, then took a box from the pile and handed it to her. She opened it to find a pink mohair sweater. Lifting it out of the box, she held it close.

"Oh, Bill, it's beautiful," she whispered.

"It's like you . . . soft and pink," he said, wanting to reach out and touch her glowing cheek. Instead he handed her another box.

In it she found a pink and gray wool skirt. In a third box were gray, leather, high-heeled shoes in her size. She looked at him with a puzzled expression.

"Where did you ever learn how to buy clothes for a woman? Color coordinated, at that!"

"Uh, well, I'd rather not say." He looked down self-consciously. "But I do want you to know that I haven't bought anything like that for anyone for over two years," he added hastily.

She smiled. "I know . . . since you became a Christian."

"Yeah." His boyish grin made her heart skip a beat.

"I saved this for last." He handed her a small box.

She opened it to find a dainty gold heart on a gold chain. She frowned. Closing the box, she set it on the coffee table.

"What's wrong?" Bill asked.

"It's just too much, that's all. I appreciate the clothes. I'll feel better going to the doctor with Billy if I can look nice." How could she explain to him that a gift of jewelry was too personal? True, they had been married, but all the years in between had taken too much out of the relationship.

Bill shrugged with disappointment, then tucked the box into his jacket pocket. Maybe he could change her mind later. At least she accepted the clothes.

After Janice changed, she sat on Billy's bed and gently shook him. "Time to get up, honey. You have a doctor's appointment."

Billy rolled over. "Hey, Mom, you look like an angel," he said, rubbing his eyes. Then he frowned. "Where did you get that sweater?" he demanded, fully awake now.

"It doesn't matter. Just hurry and get up. You'll be late for your appointment."

"*He* got it for you, didn't he?" Billy shouted. "Give it back! We aren't his family. We don't need him! And I'm not going to the doctor!" He flung himself out of bed and pulled on his jeans and shirt.

Bill entered the room and said, "I just ordered breakfast. It will be here soon."

"We don't want your breakfast, and we don't want your clothes!" Billy shouted at him.

"Please, Billy, calm down," Janice urged, taking his arm. "I know you're upset, but this doctor's appointment is important—it affects the rest of your life."

"I don't want to go!" The angry boy shook himself loose from her grasp, knocking her off balance.

"Billy!" she exclaimed.

"That's enough, Billy," Bill said with quiet firmness.

"Don't tell me what to do! Don't you ever tell me what to do!" Billy swung his arm and knocked over the table lamp. "Who do you think you are, giving me orders?"

Bill took one long stride to reach Billy, gripped him by the arms, and lifted him off the floor.

"I am your father," he said coldly. "And you'd better get used to it." For a moment the two glared at each other with identical expressions, until Bill finally lowered his son to the floor. Billy stepped away, trembling but still defiant.

"Stop it! Both of you, stop it!" Janice cried. She flung herself into the ornate bedroom chair.

"Mom, I'm sorry. Please don't cry." Billy rushed over to her and knelt beside the chair. "I'll go to the doctor. I will. But please don't make me talk to . . . to him!"

But Janice continued to cry. Billy had never needed discipline. He had never acted this way before.

Bill was not certain his actions had been appropriate, but he decided not to back down. "Billy, get ready to go," he said.

Billy glared at Bill, then went into the bathroom and slammed the door.

Bill knelt beside Janice, his arm around her shoulder.

"I'm sorry this happened," he said. "Please don't shut me out again. I have Billy's best interest at heart—I promise."

Janice sat up, brushing away her tears with the handkerchief he gave her. "I know you do. But please don't hit him. He's really a good boy."

Bill pulled back in alarm at her words, then realized how his actions must have looked to her.

He caressed her face with his hands. "Sweetheart, I promise you . . ."

A knock on the door interrupted him. Reluctantly he rose to answer.

The waiter wheeled in a cart loaded with ham, eggs, coffee, pastries, juice, milk, and cereal. Bill tipped him, declining his offer to serve them at the table in the dining area.

Soon Billy slouched at the table nibbling a pastry, and Bill toyed with his food. Janice could not eat at all. She sipped some coffee, then paced the room, waiting for time to pass. Her eyes focused for the first time on the large arrangement of pink roses Bill had ordered. She glanced at the fruit basket with the cast-aside pewter figures. Bill had gone to so much trouble to make this an enjoyable trip for them. He had taken important time away from his football practice in the middle of the season when he could have simply written her a check and left it up to her to make all the arrangements with the doctor. He wanted to be involved. He truly wanted to help.

Janice remembered the hurried trip from home the night before in George's truck. She thought about the bumper sticker in the cab and her prayer for God's help. *God answered that prayer*, she thought. Even though Billy had run away, they had found him quickly. Maybe God would work everything else out too. Maybe He could be trusted. She smiled to herself at the memory of the wonderful peace that had filled her when she prayed.

God, I'm going to trust You again, she prayed silently, and she felt the same tranquillity enfold her. She sat at the table and began to eat, unaware of the soft glow on her face.

Bill saw the change, and his appetite improved immediately. Billy, on the other hand, became even more sullen than before.

The three arrived at the doctor's office only a few minutes late. Janice filled out the necessary forms, glancing up with amusement as the nurse and receptionist fussed over Bill while he signed his autograph for them. Then the nurse took Billy into a back room to X-ray his legs. In a few minutes she invited Bill and Janice to join their son in the examining room.

Dr. Klein came into the room with the X-rays in hand and inserted them in the viewing screen. After friendly introductions, he showed them before and after pictures of children who had had an osteotomy, the surgery Billy needed. Some had healed better than others. Dr. Klein assured them that Billy's excellent health made success likely. He set the date for the operation—the first Wednesday in December, so Bill could be there between games.

Billy liked Dr. Klein. The doctor spoke to him as an adult, yet explained the surgery in terms easy to understand. The bone of his left lower leg, called the tibia, would be cut. The leg would then be secured by pins through the bone connected to a frame on the side of his leg. The frame would then be slowly adjusted one millimeter each day until his left leg was as long as his right leg. Billy would not be able to bear weight on his left leg for at least six weeks. He would then walk on crutches and have physical therapy for months afterwards.

Dr. Klein, a longtime fan of Bill and of the Mavericks, took the time to give them a tour of the operating room at nearby Children's Hospital, where the surgery would take place.

Billy shuddered at the memory of his last hospital stay. When he saw Bill eyeing him, he stiffened. He would not show his fear again, especially in front of *him*. At the same time, he decided he would do whatever it took to please his mother. He felt guilty for shoving her away that morning. But he moved away from Bill whenever he came close.

No wonder his mother had lied to him about who his father was, he thought. Big Buck Mason! He had deserted and disowned them, and now he was coming around trying to make up for it. But it was too late. They didn't need him. He would have the operation for his mother's sake, but he never wanted to see his father again. The only thing that confused him was the way his mother accepted the guy. Why did she keep smiling at him that way?

They left Denver early that afternoon. Bill drove them home rather than flying back to L.A., because he wanted to spend as much time as possible with them. In Colorado Springs, they stopped at a hamburger drive-through and ordered lunch. Billy refused to answer Bill's question about what he wanted, so Janice ordered a large burger and root beer for him. She frowned at her son for his rudeness, but he just kept staring out the window.

Bill was undaunted by Billy's coolness. At least their father-son relationship was out in the open; and better yet, Janice had warmed up to him. That was enough for now.

At the trailer, Billy disappeared into his room without a word. As Bill and Janice sat on the couch in the living room, they heard the sound of paper being torn angrily.

"He's ripping up the posters," Bill said.

"Yeah . . . I know. He's going to be sorry someday," Janice said. "It's really good of you to go on with everything in spite of the way Billy is acting."

"Janice, he's my son," Bill answered. "Besides, that's the example I see in my heavenly Father. No matter how rotten I act, He still loves me and takes care of me."

"Like the father of the prodigal son," she said.

"Yeah, that's right."

"You know, I've been thinking . . ." she went on, "it was really bad of me to go off and leave my mother like I did. I could have at least written to her. I never even gave her a thought."

Bill waited as she struggled for words.

"Lying to Billy about who his father was . . . that was wrong, too. None of this would have happened if I had just told him the truth. I've always thought I was a good person, but I've done a lot of wrong things." She paused again, then added, "I think I need to be saved."

Bill didn't move. This was so unexpected. Why couldn't he think of anything to say? Shouldn't he quote a Bible verse or something?

"I read in this Bible," Janice said, picking up the Bible from the coffee table, "that while we were still sinners, Christ died for us." She turned the pages but could not find the verse. "Do you know where it says that?"

"No. No, I don't. Try John chapter three, verse sixteen. That's a good one."

"I know that one from when I was a kid. Isn't that the one that says 'whosoever believes in Jesus has everlasting life'?"

"Yeah, that's the one," Bill said.

"Well, I'm a sinner, and I believe in Jesus. What else?" she said.

Bill cleared his throat. "Uh, well, you can thank Him for dying for you and tell Him you believe in Him."

Janice bowed her head and closed her eyes. "God, I believe in You and in Jesus. I know I'm a sinner. So, thank You that Jesus died for me." She paused, wanting to get it right. "Is that all?"

Bill nodded, unable to speak.

"Am I saved?"

He nodded again, his eyes shining with tears.

"Don't I have to do anything?" she asked.

When Bill could find his voice, he said, "There are lots of

things you'll want to do now that you're saved. But Jesus did all the work to save us. We just have to receive the free gift. That's all there is to it."

She smiled. "I'm taking the free gift right now. I'm not going to pass it up any longer."

Bill reached over and pulled her close. "O God, thank You for saving Janice. Lord, how I thank You! Please save Billy, too."

For several minutes he held her close, and she rested in his arms. He wished this golden moment could go on forever. But checking the clock in the kitchen, he saw he would have to hurry to catch his plane. How he hated to leave! Reluctantly he pulled back from Janice.

"I'm going to tell Billy good-bye," he said, and he walked down the trailer hallway to his son's door. He tapped on the door, but there was no answer.

"Billy, whether you believe it or not, I love you. We're going to get this worked out." He paused, but Billy did not respond. "Good-bye, son. I'll see you in about two weeks."

At the door, he kissed Janice on the forehead and started out, then turned back.

"I almost forgot something real important." He reached into his jacket pocket. "This check is made out to you. Just take it— no arguments," he said sternly when she began to protest. "I want you to get a telephone so we can keep in touch. Here is my number." He handed her a slip of paper. "My answering service will always know where I am. Will you do that?"

Janice sighed. "Okay . . . I guess so. Thanks."

Bill gazed into her eyes. "You're beautiful, Janice."

She laughed and looked down, shaking her head.

"I wish you could see yourself like I do," he said. He lifted her chin and gently kissed her on the lips.

A confused frown crossed her face, and she pulled back. "Bill!"

"Now that you're a Christian, we'll have a lot to talk about," he said quickly, afraid the kiss had spoiled things.

She nodded, a slight smile reappearing on her face.

He continued to look at her.

"You're going to miss your plane," she whispered.

He didn't move.

"Bill, get out of here," she said with a laugh.

He walked slowly to his car, then turned and waved before getting in.

Janice laughed again when she heard him shout, "Yahooo!" as he drove away.

TWELVE

Mac Devine returned on Saturday with Frankie, Alice, and their infant son. The borrowed truck and the rented U-Haul trailer were both filled with furniture and personal belongings to furnish their rented mobile home, not far from Janice's place. Mac had told his son about Janice and Billy and their connection with football star Buck Mason. When they phoned Gracie from West Virginia, she told them all that had happened to Janice, Buck, and Billy.

Janice was as joyful about the reunion of her friends' family as they were. She looked forward to meeting the young couple, hoping they could answer some of the questions that had come to her mind since Wednesday night.

When they finally met and Billy and Janice greeted the couple, Frankie said, "So this is Buck Mason, Jr. You look just like your daddy, kid!"

"I'm Billy Griffin!" The boy extended his hand to Frankie without any further comment.

Alice had an outgoing personality and was a delight to her mother-in-law. The baby won everyone's affection—except Billy's.

On Sunday Janice helped Alice unpack. As Alice dug through boxes searching for cooking utensils and bedding, Janice washed dishes and put them in the cupboard. She kept looking for an opportunity to ask some questions, but Alice was a whirlwind of busyness. Finally the two women took a break, and Janice had her chance.

"Alice, I just got . . . uh . . . saved the other night. Do you know what that means?"

"Sure do. I'm a Christian, too, Jan. Got saved when I was in high school. Frankie got saved in prison. Wait till you hear his story. It'll curl your hair!" Alice bubbled. "I'm really glad for you. Isn't Jesus the greatest?"

"I guess so. I mean, sure. But I don't know much about Him. I try to read my Bible, but a lot of it doesn't make sense yet. My ex-husband tells me it will take time," Janice said.

"Oooeee! Honey, I can't believe you were married to Buck Mason! He is so gorgeous! He's so good-looking, he should just be a picture on a wall. What did you let him get away for?"

"Well, it was a long time ago. We were just kids," Janice said.

Alice quickly became contrite. "There I go, popping off again. I'm sorry. I keep asking the Lord to do guard duty on my tongue. Besides, it's not what's on the outside, it's what's on the inside of somebody that counts, right?"

"Buck . . . Bill, I mean, is really a nice person. But I honestly don't know him very well. We hadn't seen each other for ten years. He's different now that he's a Christian," Janice said.

"Do you think you'll get together with him again?" Alice's eyes grew big. "How romantic!"

Janice smiled at her new friend's enthusiasm but did not answer. *No,* she thought, *I don't think we'll be getting together.*

After a few minutes Alice said, "Well, I guess since you're a new baby in the Lord, I'll have to start feeding you some baby food."

Janice looked at her. "What?"

"That's Bible talk for growing in the Lord. Have you got a Bible? Where do you go to church?"

"Church?"

"Sure, honey. Don't you go to church? Oh, maybe you don't know a good church yet, since you're just newly saved. Oh well. Frankie and me will find a good one in town and take you with us."

Janice was not sure she liked the idea, but she said nothing. Talking with Alice was like talking with a cyclone. But she was fun, too. There was a spirit about her that attracted Janice. Though she had always found it hard to trust people, she found herself thinking of Alice as a friend. *Maybe learning to trust people is a benefit of being a Christian,* she thought.

Billy soon forgave Frankie for calling him Buck Mason, Jr. He desperately needed a replacement for his former hero, so he latched onto the ex-convict, imagining there must be something exciting and dangerous about a man who had been in prison.

Eager to spend time with his new friend, he welcomed Frankie's offer to teach him wood carving. On Monday, after school, Frankie brought his tool kit to the trailer for a lesson.

"Man, that's a cool kit you got there," Billy said.

"Check it out, kid," Frankie said. "Just be careful of the blades."

Billy examined the various tools with interest.

"Here's a pattern book," Frankie said. "Find something you want to carve. If it's not too complicated for a first try, I'll show you how to get started."

Billy thumbed through the large book. His eyes spotted a football figure, and he opened the book wider.

"Yeah, that's a good one," Frankie said, tapping the page.

But Billy flipped the page and found a horse to carve instead.

As the lessons progressed, Billy questioned Frankie about his prison experience. "I guess you met some pretty cool dudes in there," he said.

Frankie snorted in disgust "If they was so cool, they wouldn't be dumb enough to be in prison. It ain't like you see on TV, kid."

"They show some pretty rough stuff sometimes," the boy said. "Like there's always one guy who takes charge. Nobody messes with him, and he'll take care of you if he likes you. If he don't, then look out." Billy grinned as he pantomimed drawing his carving tool across his throat.

Frankie stopped his carving and stared for a moment at Billy. "Kid, I'm gonna set you straight on how it really is in there." He told him several stories from his own experience, leaving only the worst details to the boy's imagination.

"Man!" Billy gasped, "What a trip! How did you make it through?"

"Lots of prayer, kid, lots of prayer."

Billy set his jaw. He would not listen to any God-talk. "Yeah, well, I'm having trouble with the back legs on this horse. Maybe I'd better take a break and get back to it tomorrow." He began packing up the tools.

"Sure," Frankie said. *Poor kid*, he thought. *He's in prison, and he don't even know it. Lord, please set him free soon.*

Each day Janice tapped the reservoir of Alice's Bible knowledge. While Billy and Frankie carved at her trailer, she studied at Alice's trailer while the baby slept.

"It's amazing how up-to-date the Bible is," Janice said one day.

"That's 'cause it's God's Word, honey. And God knows the whole story from start to finish," Alice stated.

"I'm starting to understand things that didn't make sense just two weeks ago," Janice added.

"Oh, Jan, honey, did you know that God's Holy Spirit came to live inside you the very second you asked Jesus to be your Savior?"

"He did?"

"Yes, He sure did. He lives inside you now so He can teach you. Every time you sit down to read, you need to ask Him to show you what God wants you to learn that day. You'll be surprised at how many times the very things that happen to you in a day will be what God told you about in your quiet time."

"To quote my son's favorite word, 'Wow,'" Janice said. "To think of all the years I've wasted trying to run my own life . . ."

"I know what you mean," Alice went on. "Say, what do you hear from your ex?"

"He calls every night."

"And?" Alice inquired, a grin spreading across her face.

"Oh, stop it," Janice said laughing. "We only talk about spiritual things."

"Uhh-huh." Alice nodded, but her face showed amused disbelief.

"Listen, Alice, what I really need help with is . . ." She paused, looking down. It was hard to say. "Calling my mother."

"Oh, poor kid. How long has it been?"

"I haven't talked to her in over ten years. I don't even know her. Never did. She was always drunk. Or so it seems. I don't even know who paid for the house or food."

"What about your dad?"

"I don't know. My mother cried any time I asked about him. My brother Pete once told me he died, but I think he ran off," Janice said.

"How sad for her," Alice said. "Either way, it had to be bad."

Janice stared at her. "I know . . . I know. I feel so guilty about running off with Billy. One thing I do remember is how she struggled to be alert when I brought him around. She really loved him. And here I took away her last bit of joy." She sighed. "I wish there was something I could do."

"You have a phone. Call her," Alice said.

Janice laughed. "It's that simple, isn't it? Call her. Alice, you have a way of getting right to the heart of things. Will you come home with me while I do it?"

"Sure. Let me grab the little tiger. I think he's awake now."

When they got to her place, Janice was glad Billy was away doing his chores for his elderly friends. This was not a conversation she wanted him to hear. She sat beside Alice on the couch and phoned information for Theodore, Alabama. Then she punched in the numbers and squeezed Alice's hand.

Margaret Griffin sat in her living room planning the

Christmas party for her singles Sunday school class. As her pencil traced the list of people she would be calling on for help, her eyes lit on her friend Janice Reed's name. As so often happened, she remembered her own Janice, and the negative thoughts came to life again. The drunk years she remembered so poorly. Albert deserting her. Pete dying, maybe without even being saved. Precious baby Billy taken away by sweet, gentle Janice whose patience with her had finally worn out.

No! She would not do this to herself. Jesus Christ had forgiven her. These thoughts were not from Him. Besides, dear Bill had told her that Janice had recently become a Christian. Surely she would be calling soon.

Margaret smiled as she remembered the years she had prayed for Bill, watching every televised game he played. When she read in a Christian magazine that he had become a Christian, she prayed for further miracles and soon he came to ask for her help in finding Janice. The two had searched the few things Janice had left behind. A copy of her Social Security card told them that she had not changed her name on her official records when they married. That was why no Janice Mason could be found.

The sudden, sharp ring of the telephone startled Margaret. As she had done for years at such times, she prayed, *Lord, please let it be my Janice*. But when she answered, there was only silence.

"Hello. Is someone there? Hello?"

"Mother? I mean, is this Margaret Griffin?"

Tears began to rise as relief and happiness flooded Margaret's heart.

"Janice . . . Yes, this is your mother. I'm . . . I'm so glad you called. How are you? How is Billy?"

"Billy's fine, eh, Mother. He's real big—big and strong, like Bill."

"That's wonderful. Bill told me about my grandson's accident. I'm sorry. Thank God, something can be done about it," Margaret said.

"Mother . . ." Janice said. "*Mother* . . . it feels so good to call you Mother . . . I—I love you." Janice paused. Both women struggled to speak clearly as tears streaked their faces.

"Mother, will you please . . . please forgive me for going away and hurting you?"

"Oh, my darling Janice," Margaret sobbed, "will *you* please forgive *me?*"

Mother and daughter talked at length, at first trying to condense the happenings of ten years into one brief conversation, and finally realizing today was just the beginning of their new relationship.

"Janice, I would love to come and visit you. Would that be all right?" Margaret said.

"Come visit?" Janice glanced around her simple trailer. It was so plain—certainly not the kind of place you could show off to your mother!

Alice, still beside her, seemed to understand her dilemma and whispered, "It ain't your *house* she wants to see, Janice."

"Oh yes, Mother, please visit us. I would love to see you. When can you come?"

"I have some leave time coming up at the end of the year. Let me check at work to see which days I can take off, okay?" Margaret said.

"Make it soon if you can, Mother."

When they finally hung up, Janice hugged Alice happily as a proxy for her distant mother. "If I had known how wonderful it is to be saved, I would have become a Christian ages ago!" she said.

Alice beamed at her. "I know exactly what you mean."

THIRTEEN

Billy had mixed feelings about his surgery. He wasn't afraid of the pain. He often had backaches because his shorter left leg caused the muscles and backbone to twist unnaturally as he walked. But Dr. Klein had been optimistic about the surgery, so Billy dared to dream that someday he might be able to play sports at school. That thought lessened his concern about the temporary discomfort of the brace he would be wearing.

Billy's deepest anxiety concerned seeing Buck Mason again. Why did his mother insist that man could be there? The NFL hotshot didn't deserve to be acting like a father now, after he had ignored them for so many years. And his mother actually tried to take some of the blame. She hadn't done anything wrong. A father was supposed to be there for his family! Why hadn't he cared enough to try to see them sooner?

As far as Billy was concerned, all Buck's talk about God made it even worse. If that was the way Christians treated people, Billy would *never* be a Christian. But then again Frankie was a Christian, and he was cool. And now his own mother was a Christian. But she had always been a good person anyway. It just didn't make any sense. All Billy knew was that he would throw up if he saw his mother smile at Buck one more time.

Meanwhile, Bill took the matter of his delinquent child support payment seriously. In addition to paying the remainder of Billy's earlier hospital bill, he began to send weekly checks to Janice. When she protested, he reminded her that he owed her twelve thousand dollars. He won her over only because she decided to save some money for Billy's college education.

Now for the first time in her life Janice could spend some money on herself without feeling guilty. She bought several dresses, with Alice's help, but mostly bought her favorite clothing items—jeans and shirts.

To Gracie's delight, Janice began to eat better too. Her face took on a younger, smoother appearance, and she began wearing moderate amounts of makeup. Her newfound happiness in her salvation and her improved health brought a glow to her face and a spring to her step that turned the heads of the customers she waited on daily.

Janice and Billy were scheduled to meet Bill at Denver's Majestic Inn on the first Tuesday in December. Bill flew in from his game in New York. Janice couldn't bring herself to fly, so she and Billy took a bus from Pueblo and then a cab from the bus station in downtown Denver to the hotel.

Christmas was in the Denver air when they arrived. Janice knew this would be the best Christmas of her life because she finally understood what it meant that Jesus Christ had been born into this world. She prayed every day that Billy would come to the same understanding.

At the hotel she enjoyed the deferential treatment they received. The doorman bowed, the bellhop hastened to take her bags, and the snobbish desk clerk had no idea this attractive young woman was the same one who had hopped out of a cattle truck only a few weeks before.

They were ushered into an eighth-floor suite with a mountain view. Flowers and fruit awaited them, and on the coffee table sat a football. Billy went to it and picked it up. All the Mavericks players had autographed it. They had also sent a card wishing him a speedy recovery. Billy examined the football, reading each name and picturing the player who had signed it just for him! But when he saw Janice watching him, he quickly shoved it away and turned on the television.

Bill arrived later that day. He was tired from the previous night's game and the long flight across the country. But jet lag was not new to him. He knew he would bounce back by morning. His major concern was how to handle Billy. He did not want to make any more mistakes. He had talked to his pastor and had read several books on Christian parenting, but there was no precedent for their particular situation. Unlike football, where he could plan a play and make it work to perfection, he was not gaining any yardage toward his goal of reconciliation with his son.

Janice was another story. He was confident she would marry him now that she was a Christian. True, she had been reluctant to talk about their personal relationship on the phone, but he attributed that to her shyness. Once they were together and he showed her the ring he had bought, he was sure she would say yes. He'd been dreaming about the house they would buy, perhaps a ranch, near enough to Los Angeles to keep him close to the Mavericks' facilities. Janice could choose a private Christian school for Billy. Before summer, Bill could begin to make up for all the lost years.

Late that afternoon, he knocked on the door of Janice and Billy's suite, and when Janice answered, he stepped forward to embrace her. Her eyes widened, and she quickly stepped back, holding out her hand for him to shake.

"Hi," she said, a shy smile showing her goodwill toward him.

"Hi. It's good to see you." He held her small hand between his two large ones.

"It's good to see you, too." She gently withdrew her hand, looking down at the floor.

"May I come in?"

She laughed. "Oh, yes . . . of course. Come in." She glanced at the flowers on the dining table. "Thank you for the beautiful flowers. They're, uh, beautiful." She laughed at her own awkwardness. "And thank you for the football. It was so nice of everyone to sign it."

"That was from the Broncos game," he said, looking toward Billy in hopes of sparking his interest. "The sixty-yard pass . . ."

"Billy, did you hear that?" Janice looked over at her son, who sat slumped on the couch, deliberately engrossed in an old western rerun on television. When he didn't answer, she turned to Bill to apologize. But he just smiled and shook his head to show it was all right.

Janice looked at Bill as she said, "We have to be at the hospital at 5 this evening to get Billy admitted and to have another X-ray and get some lab work done. Then . . . oh, I almost forgot—I wanted to tell you that they have one of those houses for parents next door to the hospital. They have an opening there for the next few days. I'll be staying there." Janice wondered how Bill would react to this news.

"I figured it would be more comfortable for you to stay here at the hotel," Bill said, frowning. Then he whispered, "Will you at least stay here tonight after Billy is asleep at the hospital? I'd like to take you to dinner. Something very special."

Janice bit her lower lip and glanced over at Billy, then back at Bill. His expression was just like her son's when he wanted his own way.

Bill took her hand, his dimpled smile making it difficult for her to look at him. "Please?" he said.

She looked down, a shy smile quivering at the corner of her mouth. He was doing so much for them and asking for so little. She nodded her assent.

"Let me get our things together," she said and disappeared into the bedroom.

Bill sat on the couch beside Billy and cleared his throat. What should he say? Billy stood up and moved to a chair. After a brief delay Bill commented, "That was my favorite show when I was your age. I've even met the actor who plays the marshall. Would you like to meet him someday?"

Billy grabbed the remote control from the table and clicked the buttons until he found a cartoon show.

Bill glanced toward the bedroom door, wishing Janice would hurry. How could he reach Billy? It was hard for the rugged quarterback to wait and hope, not knowing what else to do. He shook his head and prayed silently, *Father, please make something happen in Billy's life that will help him get over his bitterness toward me and toward You. God, I would give up everything, even football, to have my son's forgiveness and for him to have Yours!*

Arriving at the hospital by cab, they were quickly surrounded by many more nurses and attendants than necessary because of Buck Mason's fame. The attention made Janice uncomfortable. Billy was sullen and withdrawn. The nurses, both young and old, fluttered around like mother hens. As they checked the boy in, they eyed the handsome quarterback.

Billy gripped his mother's hand for the first time in years. The surgery that had seemed so far in the future was now looming like a frightening giant right in front of him. He squeezed his mother's fingers tightly when the young man from the lab drew blood from his other arm. He relaxed a little when Dr. Adams, the anesthesiologist, introduced herself and made friendly conversation while she checked Billy's medical records. Dr. Klein put in an appearance to answer any last-minute questions they had.

Billy could not eat much of the light supper brought to him. By 8 o'clock, exhausted from the ordeal, he fell asleep. Janice felt guilty leaving him alone, but the nurse promised to check on him frequently.

Bill and Janice took a cab back to the hotel and went to their respective rooms to change for dinner. Janice put on a pink chiffon dress Alice had talked her into buying. Bill dressed in a black western suit and boots. A silver and turquoise belt buckle matched the bolo tie he wore with the pale blue-green western shirt. The suit matched his black hair, and the aqua of the shirt reflected in his eyes, intensifying their color. Nervous about their evening, not sure she was ready to admit, even to herself, how she really felt about Bill, Janice could hardly look at him. And when she did, she blushed, and her cheeks glowed becomingly.

"The dining room here is famous for its seafood and its view of the mountains," Bill commented as they took the elevator to the top-floor restaurant. "The seafood is flown in fresh every day. I always come here when I'm in Denver. Do you like seafood?"

"I've never had much. Does tuna fish count?" she asked.

Bill laughed. "I'll order for you."

Janice looked up into his brilliant eyes and caught her breath. Was there ever a more handsome man on the face of the earth? she wondered as her heart fluttered wildly.

At that moment the elevator stopped, and Janice, unaccustomed to either elevators or high-heeled shoes, was forced to grip Bill's arm so she wouldn't fall when her heel caught in the track of the sliding door.

"Oh!" she cried softly, embarrassed and confused. Bill just smiled as he helped her regain her balance, and her heart danced wildly again.

The grandeur of the hotel had staggered Janice from the first time she'd seen it. Now she gaped at the elegant dining room. The walls were hung with red brocade wallpaper and were bordered by dark wood. Black, wrought-iron sconces held dark red candles that gave a romantic Spanish look to the large room. Paintings and sculptures of *conquistadores* and Spanish dancers graced the walls. Expensive red linen cloths covered the tables, and red, embroidered napkins were set at each place. No paper or plastic here, she noticed. Even the menus were printed on heavy parchment. And just as Bill promised, floor-to-ceiling windows showed a breathtaking panoramic view of the snow-covered mountains and the Christmas-lit city.

The maitre d' showed them to their table. Janice, used to waiting on people in an informal diner, felt uncomfortable being served, especially with so much ceremony. She feared she would do something foolish. But she could not resist staring at the elegance of the room.

An orchestra played softly on the opposite side of the room from their secluded corner booth. Several couples moved gracefully about on the red-tiled dance floor. The booth was quiet, and the soft candlelight gave an air of romance.

Bill watched Janice to see if she was impressed. This booth was a good choice—private but with a good view of the windows, stage, and dance floor. He wanted her to see that he would always order the best of everything for her.

Janice tried to fade into the corner of the booth. She squirmed as the maitre d' and waiters kept hovering about, checking her every need. This was not her world! She did not belong here! But Bill looked right at home.

After ordering dinner, he slid closer to her, took her hand, and raised it to his lips.

"Janice, you are one beautiful woman. Pink makes your face glow, just like an angel's." His blue eyes sparkled in the candlelight, and Janice looked down to avoid his intense gaze. She pulled her hand back and moved away from him.

"It's okay. Nobody can see us here," he said. "Don't pull away." He leaned forward to kiss her.

"Bill, don't!" she warned.

"I'm sorry, sweetheart. It's just that I love you. I want you to marry . . ."

"No! Don't say that!" Tears sprang to her eyes.

Confusion and concern filled his eyes. "But . . . why? Everything's going to be okay now. Look how far we've come. A lot of people are praying for us, and Billy's going to come around soon. I can feel it. We can be a family again. Hey, don't cry."

"Why can't you understand?" she whispered. "We live in . . . in different worlds."

"But we're both Christians now. That puts us in the same world," he said. "Come on now. Don't you want us to be a family so we can . . ."

"No." She avoided his eyes while she spoke. "I . . . I know when we were married I was very . . . uh, domestic. But I've been independent for a long time. Now that you're helping with Billy's expenses, I want to get back into college."

"I won't stop you. That would be great. If that's what you want to do . . ."

"It's not the same. I need to make my own decisions. I don't like to answer to anyone. I want to learn more about the Bible . . . and myself. I've been so busy raising Billy, I don't even know who I am." She ventured a look at Bill. He was sitting back in the booth with a boyish pout on his face.

"Stop that!" she said. "When you look like that, I get so confused . . ."

He sat up, grinning, and reached into his pocket to pull out a gray, velvet ring box.

"Let me show you what I bought for you," he offered. "Maybe this will straighten out your confusion."

"I don't want to see it. And please stop looking at me like that," she responded, turning to look away.

"Like what?" he asked, laughing.

"Like a . . . like you're a movie star . . . or Mr. America! Like a Greek god. Don't you understand? When you look at me, my feelings become so confused I can't think straight. What woman wouldn't be dazzled by you? Even Alice thinks you're something out of a dream. How would I ever know if I wanted to marry you because of who you really are? I don't even *know* who you really are. But I do know I don't want to be married to someone that every woman in America daydreams about!" Janice sat back and twisted her napkin.

It was Bill's turn to squirm. "I can't believe you're serious," he said. He played with the ring box for a moment, then shot her a serious look. "Are you sure that's the real reason?"

"What other reason would there be?" She ventured another glance in his direction, and her heart did somersaults as she watched the struggle in his face.

"It's not other women daydreaming about me that bothers you. It's me thinking of other women . . . like before. My . . . my infidelity. You don't trust me, do you? You don't think I'll be faithful to you."

His wounded look made her heart soften. She reached out to touch his hand. "Bill, I know you're different from the way you were ten years ago. I understand now. I really do. Remember, the Lord is changing me, too." Her voice fell to a whisper, and she looked down again, retrieving her hand before he misunderstood. "I . . . just . . . I just don't love you."

As the words sank in, a small, hollow ache replaced the joy that had filled his heart for days in anticipation of this night.

"You really mean that, don't you?" he said.

She nodded, not looking up.

"I see," he said.

In the silence that followed, he searched his own heart. Every woman he had ever pursued had been his for the asking. One smile, one hint that he was interested, had made them putty in his hands. Now when his real happiness was at stake, that winning quality seemed to chase away the only woman he wanted to love forever.

A wild moment of jealousy raced through his mind as he thought about the crude truck drivers she saw every day at the diner. But he knew that was unfair. She had never cared for them either. Maybe he had killed her ability to love . . . or rather, to be loved. He sighed with regret.

This was too much.

Lord, help me, he prayed silently.

The waiters had been bringing their meal in courses, each one more delicious than the one before. The maitre d' quietly supervised the serving of his famous guest and his companion.

Janice tried to enjoy the dinner. The shrimp cocktail and lobster tails were delicious. But she ate only a few bites of each dish. Her stomach was in knots as the waiters watched for her approval. Did they do this to everyone? she wondered. How could anyone swallow with three people standing there staring at them?

She glanced at Bill. The light had gone out of his eyes.

He caught her gaze and smiled ruefully. With difficulty, he began small talk.

"Where do you plan to go to college?"

"I can take the basic requirements at Pueblo Junior College. I'm sure that will give me a good foundation." Janice had not thought that far ahead, but it seemed like a good answer.

"I could help you," he said.

She shook her head. "No . . . That's okay."

"Do you mind if I come see you once in a while?"

"I guess not."

"Did I tell you the movie I'm in will be filmed in Taos and up by Creede? I'll be there in February for some snow scenes and then again in June. I could come over . . ."

"Tell me about the movie," she said.

"It's a comedy western with Robert Ruskin."

"Robert Ruskin! Oh, he's awful. I'd never let Billy see any of his movies."

"You wouldn't? Why not?" Bill asked.

"He's awful. He's disgusting. He makes R-rated movies and has . . . Well, he has a bad reputation."

"Hmm. To tell the truth, I never thought about all that. I haven't read the script, or signed the contract for that matter. My business manager was working on it." Bill frowned. He had agreed to do the movie early in the season, thinking of the good exposure it would give him for the future. Someday he would not be playing football, and acting sounded like a good second career.

"I guess I'd better check it out," he said. "I'd hate to damage my Christian testimony by being associated with a movie that is morally objectionable." He reached out and touched her hand. "Thanks for telling me how you feel about it."

He wanted to tell her how much he needed her discernment to balance his sometimes rash ways. But she was watching the Spanish dancers make their entrance onto the stage while the orchestra played the introduction for the floor show.

Bill and Janice were both glad that conversation was no longer necessary.

FOURTEEN

Early the next morning, they returned to the hospital to see Billy before he went into surgery. He was lying on his bed staring at the ceiling, looking small and frightened. While Bill waited at the door, Janice came close to his bed.

"You left me," Billy accused her.

"You were asleep," she said.

"Where did you go?"

"You knew I was going to stay at the hotel last night. But I'll be here from now on, honey, I promise." She looked into his fear-filled eyes and leaned over to kiss him. "Don't be afraid. It's going to be all right."

He nodded. Then he looked beyond her and saw Bill standing in the doorway. "Send him away!" he shouted.

Bill turned and disappeared down the hallway.

"Billy, please . . ." Janice began.

But before she could say more, the nurse and orderly came to prepare her son for surgery. She held his hand as they wheeled him toward the operating room on a gurney. Dr. Adams and Dr. Klein met them in the hallway, and Janice planted a last kiss on his cheek as they took him through the swinging doors.

She found Bill leaning against the counter at the nurses' station.

"I'm sorry for the way he acted," she said.

Bill smiled sadly. "Don't forget, I'm responsible for a lot of what he's doing. I deserve it. If I had just been there . . ."

"Okay, enough of that," she said. "We're both new people now, and we're going on from here." She paused, enjoying the light that came into his eyes. "Okay?"

"Okay."

They sat in a nearby waiting room but had little time to talk. A nurse from another floor came seeking Bill.

"Mr. Mason, I'm sorry to disturb you, but could I please ask a favor?" she said.

"Sure," he said, reaching into his pocket to get a pen to sign an autograph.

But the woman went on, "We have a little boy in our ward who is dying, and we don't expect him to live much longer. He loves football, and it would mean so much if you could come visit him."

Janice stared wide-eyed at Bill, but he took it in stride.

"I'd be happy to," he said. He reached out his hand to invite Janice along.

She hesitated, then took his hand and headed down the hallway with him.

On the elevator the nurse explained, "The child has cancer, so his appearance might be startling."

"I understand," Bill said. "I've seen a lot of kids like that."

Janice shuddered involuntarily.

"You okay?" Bill said, squeezing her hand.

She nodded. "I've just never seen dying . . . Well, I mean . . . You know."

"That's understandable," the nurse said. "You can watch from the doorway if you're uncomfortable."

Bright Christmas decorations adorned the children's cancer ward. The blinking lights in the large room suggested a cheer that was only temporary. Janice stood by the door as the nurse led Bill to the first bed. Even though they had been told the boy was eleven years old, he looked more like a seven-year-old.

The child looked up at the tall man who approached his bed and smiled, his eyes opening wide. Bill turned the bedside chair around and straddled it, leaning his chin on his arms so he could be at eye-level with his new friend.

"You play football!" the boy exclaimed. "You're Buck Mason!"

"That's right. What's your name?" Bill asked.

"Billy Maestas."

"I know another boy about your age named Billy," Bill said. "It's a good name."

The boy was quiet for a minute. "I like the Broncos best, but the Mavericks are pretty good. You make them a good team 'cause you're the quarterback," he said.

Bill smiled. "But where would I be without the rest of the team? We all work together."

The boy studied Bill's face for another minute, then said, "I'm going to die."

"Billy, we're all going to die someday."

"But I'm going to die soon. I have cancer, and the doctors can't make me well."

"I know," Bill said softly. "What do you think about dying?"

"I'm scared," the boy answered. "My mom says I'll go to a nice place where I can play all day. But I heard one nurse say they'll put my body in a box and bury me, and that's all there is to it."

"But what do you think?" Bill asked again.

"I want to go to the nice place."

"I know a way you can be sure to get there."

Billy Maestas's eyes lit up. "Will you tell me about it?"

Janice watched in amazement as Bill unfolded the story of God's love to the dying boy. She wondered how he would tell the boy he needed to be saved. How could this poor, sick child have ever sinned enough to need a Savior?

"So you see, Billy, even though we might be real good, we're never as good as God—never good enough to get into His perfect heaven. We're born with sin inside of us, and we can't ever do enough good to overcome it. That's why Jesus had to be born on that first Christmas. That's why He had to die. He is God's perfect Son, and He lived a perfect life, so He didn't have to die for any sins of His own. He died to get spanked, sort of, for all the wrong things *we* do because we have sin inside us. To be forgiven, all we have to do is to accept the free gift of salvation. God says that whoever believes in Jesus and asks Him for forgiveness has everlasting life."

Billy Maestas's eyes were bright and alert. "Can I have it?" he asked.

"Sure. Just tell Jesus you accept His free gift."

Silent tears fell down Janice's cheeks as she watched Bill pray with this new child of God. This was a side of him she never knew existed. Such tenderness, such warmth—her heart glowed with admiration.

As Bill continued to talk with the boy, she walked to the waiting room outside. Digging through the magazines, she found one with Bill's picture in it. She tore the page out and took it to Bill.

He looked up, smiled his appreciation, and said, "Billy, here's my picture and autograph. You can tell everyone Buck Mason is a personal friend of yours. Then I want you to tell them that Jesus Christ is your very best friend. Okay?"

The boy nodded. "I'm gonna tell my mom about Jesus. I want her to go to heaven, too." Then he closed his eyes. "I'm real tired now. Would you go tell the other kids about Jesus?"

Bill reached out and touched the boy's face. His skin felt dry and papery. Then, gently patting his new friend's hand, Bill left his bedside and began to visit the other children in the ward.

Janice had expected to nervously pace the floor during Billy's two-hour operation. Instead she spent the time with Bill in the children's cancer ward. As the morning passed, she found it easier to watch the children as Bill went from bed to bed giving encouragement to each one. Several were too young to know he was a famous quarterback. But all of them enjoyed the way he related to them. Janice recalled how easily he had made friends with Billy Maestas. *What a heartbreak it must be for him to be shut out by his own son when he loves children so much!*

Too soon for the children, Janice called Bill away to remind him they should be checking on the progress of Billy's surgery. They returned to the waiting area outside the operating room. Soon Dr. Klein came through the swinging doors, removing his surgical mask as he walked toward them. Bill and Janice rose to meet him.

"It couldn't have gone better. That's one healthy boy. Must take after you, Buck. Good, strong bones. There's no reason to think he won't have a complete recovery and play football like his father someday."

"May we see him?" Janice asked.

"He's in the recovery room right now. We'll give him a little while to come out of the anesthesia. You might want to be there then," Dr. Klein said. "I'll be checking in on him later today."

"Thanks, doc." Bill reached out to shake the doctor's hand. Then he and Janice walked toward the recovery room. A few steps down the hall, Bill stopped.

"Look, Janice, I'm going to leave now. He won't want me there when he wakes up, and I don't want to upset him. There isn't any point in my staying around." He didn't look at her but focused on the elevator at the far end of the hall. Being with the other children had intensified his desire to be close to Billy during his painful recovery. The love he felt so ready to give to his son burned in his heart. If only his son were willing to receive it . . . He had to get away.

"But . . ." Janice said. His presence had been so reassuring. She didn't want him to leave. "I . . . I'm glad you were here. You were great with those kids upstairs." She wanted to say something to make him stay but didn't know what.

"Yeah," he said, staring down at the floor. "Well, call me if you need anything." He turned and walked down the hall, his shoulders slumped forward, his hands jammed into his pockets.

Janice watched him, her heart aching for him as he disappeared behind the elevator doors. He had not even given her a parting glance, and she suddenly felt very much alone. How she wanted to follow him, to bring him back, to . . . to what? What was this knot that formed in her chest every time she tried to sort out her feelings about Bill? She didn't know. But Billy needed her now, so she walked slowly to the recovery room.

Billy recovered rapidly. Within five days Dr. Klein pronounced him ready to go home. Bill had arranged for an ambulance to drive them there, to ensure that Billy's healing leg would suffer no stress.

When they arrived at the trailer, several surprises awaited them. A hospital bed had replaced the couch in the living room to make Billy comfortable for his six-week stay in bed. A large color television with remote control stood where the old black-and-white one had. A compact disk stereo sat on a shelf by the bed, with a large selection of country CDs. No one needed to say who sent the gifts.

Frankie and Alice had decorated a small Christmas tree and placed it beside the television. The young couple welcomed mother and son home, making sure everything Billy needed was within his reach. Alice gave Billy a report on his two adopted grandmothers, whom she'd been caring for in his absence. Mrs. Walters was still spilling things in her refrigerator, and Mrs. Anderson was looking for a new pet since her cat had disappeared. Alice promised to bring both women over to see Billy when he was ready for visitors.

Frankie had bought Billy his own wood carving set and found some interesting pieces of wood for the boy to work on during his convalescence. Frankie had also constructed a lap tray that served as a work surface as well as holding the carving tools.

It was easy to do things for the agreeable boy. He was undemanding about personal needs and was brave when the thera-

pist worked on his leg brace each day. He adjusted to sitting quietly in his bed, working on school books and wood carvings, and
watching television while Janice was at work every day. He
enjoyed the visits by Frankie, Alice, Mac, and Gracie. He was
even beginning to like the baby who was always on Alice's hip
whenever she came.

But Billy vehemently vetoed his mother's suggestion that
some of his school friends might like to come and visit. By now
everyone knew his father was the famous Buck Mason, even
those who had not figured it out long before he had. He did not
want to see anyone who might ask him about that. That was a
chapter in his life he had every intention of closing—
permanently.

FIFTEEN

In the two weeks following Billy's surgery, Janice found herself missing Bill. He no longer called or wrote. Apparently when he left the hospital that day, he'd walked out of their lives for good.

She put up with a few friendly jokes from some of her truck-driving friends when she and Billy first returned home, but now even that died down. Her life was returning to normal.

Then one day an old friend who hadn't been to the diner for a while stopped by. Terrell Martin had been Gracie's favorite candidate for Janice in her matchmaking schemes. Terrell was "head-turnin' handsome," as Gracie would say. More than that, he was a good man who cared for Janice and had been asking her out for years. Janice liked him as a friend and enjoyed talking with him. Other than Mac, he was one of the few men to whom she had related well. But she had no desire to date him. Gracie would shake her head and scold her for passing up such a good catch, but Janice stuck by her decision.

That day Terrell lingered long after he should have been on the road. Watching Janice as she cleaned the counter and tables after the lunch rush, he waited until the diner was empty, then coaxed her to take a break.

After a few minutes of small talk, he said, "I've been reading about you in the newspaper. Never thought you'd show up in the sports section."

"You heard about that?"

"It'd be hard to miss it. Buck Mason is big news any day. And to think I've been a fan of his . . ." he muttered.

"When I knew him, he was a smart-aleck, high school show-off." In response to his bemused smile, she added, "He's nicer now."

"Yeah, I can tell what you think about him by the way your eyes lit up when I mentioned his name," Terrell commented. He snapped the toothpick he had been chewing and tossed it into an ashtray.

"What's that supposed to mean?" Janice asked with a little laugh. "He's just a friend now."

"Honey, don't give me that," Terrell said. "I've been asking you out for a long time 'cause I think you're . . . that you're the sweetest little gal in Colorado, New Mexico, Wyoming, and everywhere else I run my rig." He sat back, leaned his chair against the wall, and stared across the room and on out the front window. "All these years I figured that if I just kept asking, one day you'd go out with me. No wonder you always turned me down. Just by looking in your eyes, I can see you're a lady in love, and it ain't me you're in love with. It's Buck Mason. Now don't look at me like that."

"Terrell," Janice said, "you've got this all wrong."

"Ha!" he said, leaning forward. "I know you, honey. You never looked at me or nobody else like you looked when I just said the fella's name. You love Buck Mason. Now don't deny it."

Janice laughed at his suggestion and turned the conversation to other things. But inside herself she wondered . . . She had always valued his judgment. Was he seeing something she was trying to deny?

That afternoon as she watched television with Billy, she pondered Terrell's words. It was true that many men had asked her out over the years. That was a natural part of being a waitress in a diner serving lonely traveling men. But she had never once in ten years found any man to interest her—not even a good man like Terrell Martin.

She tried to analyze her feelings toward Bill. In the months since he'd shown up, she had learned to respect him because he always tried to behave as a Christian. When he failed, he humbly admitted it and tried to do better. That was not the selfish teen she had married so long ago. She had begun to look forward to his visits with girlish excitement. She had never felt that way about Terrell or anyone else.

The memory of Bill sitting in the hospital with the dying children brought tears to her eyes. He was so gentle and tenderhearted. Since the beginning, he had done everything possible to win her trust and make up for the past. When she thought of how sad he looked as he left the hospital, the tears began to flow down her cheeks. How she wanted to go back to that day, to see him again. Sniffing softly, she reached for a tissue.

"Come on, Mom, it wasn't all that sad," Billy said, turning off the television with the remote control.

"What?"

"The TV show. It ended okay," he said.

"Oh . . . Oh, that's nice. I guess I wasn't paying attention," she said.

Billy frowned. He did not like to see his mother crying, but he was afraid to ask what had upset her. She might talk about Bug Mason, he thought, pleased with himself for his new name for Buck. He would just let her tears pass unnoticed. Soon she would forget about the creepy Bug and they would be happy again. He would make sure of it.

But Janice was becoming sure of something else. She knew she had always loved Bill, even through all those years of anger and hate. There had never been a man who could replace him in her heart. And maybe, just maybe, she had subconsciously encouraged Billy to admire the superstar who was his father. She had never allowed herself to dream he would come into her life again.

But as much as she could confess to herself that she loved Bill, she could not think of marrying him. It was not just that Billy hated him. It was the world Bill lived in. She would never fit in.

Lord, I don't know what to do. I just know I love Bill. Please help me, she prayed in childlike faith. God had answered every prayer so far, and she knew He would answer this one too.

When Bill had left the hospital the day of Billy's surgery, he was emotionally drained. It was always as tiring as it was rewarding to spend time with terminally ill children. There was so little he could do for them. But that day his personal problems had already weakened his morale.

When Janice had rejected his proposal so firmly the night before, he'd prayed silently for the Lord to help him, and peace had filled his heart in spite of the bitter disappointment. In the light of day, however, with all that was wrong between Billy and him, it was more than he could handle to remember that Janice did not love him. For the first time in his life, he felt completely defeated.

On his flight back to Los Angeles, he tried to get everything into place in his mind. The Lord seemed to be showing him over and over that there would not be an easy healing of the past. Although he knew God had forgiven his sins, he still had to fight the guilt he felt because Billy would not forgive him.

Janice had reminded him they were both new people and should forget the past and go on to the future. But the only future he wanted was with Janice and Billy, and they would not let him back into their lives.

As the plane began its descent into his home city, his depression gradually became anger over the turn of events in his life. He had never set out to hurt anyone. Some of the men in his profession were cruel and aggressive, personally as well as on the football field. Bill considered himself one of the "good guys." Why was God letting things go so wrong in his life?

Hadn't he gone to Janice to set things straight in the first place? Hadn't he paid all of Billy's medical expenses? Wasn't he willing to spend the rest of his life loving and caring for them? God could change their hearts. God could make Billy forgive him; He could make Janice love him. Was he asking too much in those few requests? Look at all the trouble he was in with Coach Speer. Look at all the expensive fines he had paid for missing practices. Besides, it wasn't like his prayers were all that selfish. He would be good for them. He would have given them a Christmas they would never forget.

Christmas! That was it. He would buy Billy the computer he wanted. That might soften him up. And he would work harder than ever with the team at the remaining practices. They had all put in extra effort this season, and now every man was at his peak, and a Super Bowl victory was within their grasp. That would win Billy over. After all, it was Bill's fame as a quarterback that had brought him his son's admiration in the first place. Anyway, he owed it to the team to not let personal problems destroy the Mavericks' chances for the NFL championship.

Before the seat belt light turned off in the plane, Bill had laid out a plan to break down Billy's wall of anger. If he could buy his son's love, maybe that would be the way to Janice's heart as well. He was so deep in thought, he did not notice the wistful sighs of several feminine flight attendants as they watched the handsome football star leave the plane.

Several days before Christmas, Bill set his plan into motion. Flying into Pueblo, he drove to the computer center where he had ordered the computer Billy liked best, then drove south to the trailer court. He sat for several minutes in the rented car, wondering what awaited him inside. He wondered if he should pray before going in, but he brushed the thought aside, as he had begun to do often lately. He could handle this without God's help. Finally, bracing himself with a deep sigh, he got out of the car, removed the cumbersome boxes from the back, and went to the door.

Billy had just finished his homework and was starting to work on his wood carving. Hearing a knock on the door, he said, "Come on in. It's open."

When he saw Bill, he frowned, rolled his eyes, and turned away. What did the Bug want? They had been doing just fine, and now he showed up to ruin everything again.

"Hello, son," Bill said as he carefully brought in the boxes containing the computer, monitor, and printer. "I brought your Christmas present. It's the kind you like. Sorry I couldn't wrap it."

Billy continued to stare out the window.

"Do you want me to open it up?" Bill asked.

Billy remained silent.

Bill watched the boy for a moment. Compassion filled his heart. The boy had had a hard life. His anger was hurting him as much as it was hurting Bill. As difficult as it might be, he would have to make his son talk about it. He sat on the edge of the hospital bed that had been placed in the living room, taking Billy's hand in the firm grip used by his teammates after a victory—a grip he knew Billy would be familiar with. But the boy's hand remained limp.

"We have to talk sooner or later, Billy."

After a long moment, Billy looked at him, his expression strangely mature yet anguished. "So what do you want?" he said.

"To be your friend . . . your father . . . To receive your forgiveness for failing you so far." Bill paused, searching his son's face for encouragement. There was none. "We were pals when I first came around, before you knew I'm your dad. I want to be your pal again."

Billy looked away. He felt calm. Yes, this was the time. He could do it. He could dump the whole load on someone else . . . on the only one who deserved it.

Turning back to Bill, he said quietly, "You think that's all there is to it, don't you? You think it's gonna be real simple to say you're sorry, and then we'll all live happily ever after. But I've got news for you—I don't want you near me or my mother ever again."

He paused, wanting to say the words, all the words, just right. As he began again, his words were measured and quiet. "You were never there all those years when all the other kids had a father and I didn't. You were never there when Mom had to work in a stinking diner where men looked at her all day. You were never there when I had to fight the guys at school who told bad lies about her. You wanna know what happened that day I fell? I was fighting those guys who talked about my mom. I chased them onto the railroad bridge, and I wanted to kill them. I hated them, and I hated God for taking my . . . my dad away. I wish He had taken you and not my Uncle Pete. I almost died, and then Mom would have been alone. And you? You never would have known or cared. It's your fault I fell. Where were you when we needed you? Big, important Buck Mason! I thought you were so great. But you're not Buck anymore. You're *Bug* Mason, a big, creepy bug!"

Billy paused, breathing hard and trembling. The searing fire in his leg was almost unbearable, but he gripped the mattress of his bed to keep from giving in to the pain.

"Billy, stop," Bill pleaded. "You're only making it worse."

"What are you gonna do, hit me?" Billy sneered.

Bill recoiled, speechless.

"I hate you," Billy said. "I want you to be hurt like you hurt us." A sob escaped him, but he choked it back. "Where were you all that time, big man?" he shouted.

Bill shuddered and shook his head, brushing away the tears that clouded his vision. "I don't know, Billy. I don't know. But I'm here now. Give me a chance," he whispered.

"No. I hate you. You don't deserve a chance."

Billy looked out the window again. After a few deep breaths to regain control of himself, he turned back to the Bug. "I never said anything to anybody about this . . . Not even Mac or Frankie. If you tell my mom, I'll . . ." He searched for the right words. "I'll get you somehow." Then he turned to the window again, hoping that looking away would make the object of his hatred disappear.

Bill felt sick to his stomach. Billy's hatred was carved in granite—it was completely unchangeable. What was worse, his reasons made sense. There was nothing Bill could do to change either the past or his son's hatred. It was over. Once he had not wanted them, and now they did not want him. All his dreams for them as a family, all his plans to make their lives better, had evaporated right in front of him. He had never been rejected in his life, and now . . . ! Well, he was finished with the whole situation. He would not go through this again.

He walked to the door, looking back for one last glance at his son. "Good-bye, Billy," he whispered.

Christmas had nearly arrived, and with the season came a feeling of goodwill and kindness. Mac and Gracie were especially joyful this year, because Frankie and his family were there. Customers were more generous with tips, neighbors were more friendly, and Janice looked forward to the first Christmas in her life when she would understand why Jesus Christ had been born into the world. Her trust in the Lord was growing, and the love she felt for Bill begged to be let out of her heart.

And she was ready to tell him! She would call him after work today. Somehow God would work out the differences in their lifestyles. After all, Bill had said he preferred simple living. The warm Colorado sunshine pierced the cool breeze and filled Janice's soul with happiness as she walked home, practicing the words she would say to the man she loved.

As she turned past the first trailer in her row, her eyes rested on the strange car in her driveway. Bill was here! She quickened her pace, her heart pounding at the thought of seeing him again, of declaring her love to him in person. She could look into those wonderful, understanding eyes and tell him she was sorry for hurting him, that she wanted to be with him forever.

There he was . . . coming out of the trailer, getting into the car. He was leaving! Had he planned to come and then go away without even trying to see her? She ran to the car just as he backed up.

"Hi, stranger," she said, smiling. Then she saw the agony on his face and the set of his jaw. "Bill, what's wrong? Did something happen with Billy?"

He shook his head. "I guess I can't get it through my head that he just doesn't want me around!"

"Oh, Bill . . . I'm so sorry! Please come back in. I'll make him listen to reason. The Lord will help us."

"No, Janice," Bill said sharply. "You don't understand! Please move. I've got to go." He backed the car up and skidded in the gravel. Leaving a flurry of dust, he turned up the highway and disappeared.

Janice stood back and watched him drive away. She had never seen him like this. Did he hate her now? Her happy plan to declare her love to him suddenly seemed childish. But anger at her son quickly replaced her concern for herself and Bill. She marched into the trailer, turned off the blaring television, and glared at Billy.

"I want to know what happened with Bill, and I don't mean maybe!"

Billy tried to cover his seething emotions. "What do you mean?"

"William David Mason, Junior, don't you give me that!" Janice surprised herself by shouting at her son for the first time in his life.

Billy flinched and looked down. "You never called me that before."

"Well, I should have. It's your name, and you'd better get used to it."

A sob escaped him, but he didn't answer.

Janice turned to sit in her chair and almost tripped on the computer box beside the Christmas tree. "Oh, Billy, did he bring this to you? Now I understand. You were hateful and rude to him when he came all this way to give you a wonderful Christmas present. What am I going to do with you?"

Billy stared at his hands, ignoring the silent tears that rolled down his cheeks.

"Why are you acting this way?" Janice asked gently. She

came to his bedside and took his face in her hands, brushing aside the tears and smoothing back his unruly hair.

"Mom, I love you," he said. "Please don't make me talk about that man."

"That man is your father. He failed us in the past, but he wants to make it up to us. Why can't you forgive him?"

"I . . . I don't know."

"You hurt him badly today." Her voice broke as she spoke.

"Mom, I don't want to hurt you. Please don't cry." He looked beyond her to the boxes on the floor. "If I use the computer, will that help?"

Janice sighed. Weariness flooded her body. Her special day was ruined. Maybe her whole life! And he was talking about playing with the computer. But then again, maybe his acceptance of Bill's gift was a start. She shrugged. "I'll get it out."

She knelt down and checked one box for instructions. It appeared very complicated in the picture. As she reached to open the end of the box, her arm brushed the Christmas tree, and a small, brightly wrapped gift fell to the floor. Picking it up, she read the attached card:

> My dearest Janice,
> My heart belongs to you,
> and it always will.
> Love, Bill.

Inside she found the delicate gold heart and chain he had bought in Denver. He still loved her! How could she have thought he was so shallow as to forget her in three short weeks? She took the pendant from the box and put it on. It was the first piece of jewelry she had owned since pawning her wedding ring after their divorce.

Janice longed to tell Bill she loved him. But he had been terribly upset when he left. She decided to let him get over today's incident. Then she would call him. And she would continue to pray for Billy and to talk to him about his horrible attitude.

SIXTEEN

In another week the Mavericks would be facing the Denver Broncos in the American Football Conference championship game. But today each team had to first go through the formality of playing lesser teams. The Mavericks would face the Omaha Aces, wild-card game winners who despite their impressive defense were not expected to score against the Mavericks because of their weak offense.

Bill always disliked playing the Aces, who had a reputation for their extreme lack of sportsmanship. They played as if each of them had a personal vendetta against every member of an opposing team. And, indeed, there was one man who hated Bill in particular.

Jared Hammer was a big, mean man. Larger than most middle linebackers, he managed to play the position well because of his great speed. His main job was to stop running plays cold, but he also loved to rush the quarterback before he could pass the ball to his receiver, and Hammer especially did the latter with frightening enthusiasm.

Hammer had been drafted by the Mavericks the same year that Bill had. But he had never succeeded on that team because of personal differences with Coach Chuck Speer, and for some reason he took it out on Buck Mason, the Mavericks' golden boy. Now that he was on a team of like-minded men, he was encouraged to do permanent damage to the health of those playing opposite him.

Janice decided to watch the game so she could see Bill. Because her large new television set had the best picture, she invited Frankie and Alice to watch the game with her that Sunday afternoon. When she announced to Billy that they would be watching the game, she expected a protest. Instead, he simply said, "Okay" and went back to his reading.

Janice would not have been so relieved by his apparent cooperation if she had known what Billy knew about Hammer's reputation. The boy looked forward to seeing him hit the hated Bug Mason with all his considerable weight and meanness. Billy even suggested they have popcorn.

Janice had never paid much attention to football. She found it boring, if not barbaric. She had tried to get interested for Billy's sake as he was growing up, but she still did not know a first down from a field goal. Yet, as she and her friends settled in front of the television, she could tell from the first few minutes that there was something not quite right about this game. One huge Ace player seemed to be running into Bill time after time with incredible power. And both Janice and Frankie noticed with dismay that Billy had a look of smug satisfaction on his face and pounded his fist into his bed triumphantly each time Bill fell to the ground beneath Hammer. Janice tried to think about the game and not her son's vengeful behavior.

Now Bill was standing on the field, his helmet in his hands. He shook his head slightly as if to clear his vision. One of his teammates spoke to him, and he looked up, waved him away, and put his helmet back on.

Janice was relieved when halftime came. She went to the kitchen to fix popcorn, and Alice joined her.

"The kid has it real bad, doesn't he?" Alice whispered.

Janice nodded wordlessly. She could not decide which upset her more—seeing Bill get hurt or seeing Billy enjoy it. How she longed for the days when Billy had worshiped Buck Mason as a hero. He'd always been a gentle boy, and this was so unlike him.

What would it take for him to forgive his father for what was just as much her fault?

The second half was even worse. "The Hammer," as the announcer called him, kept hitting Bill at every opportunity. Maverick offensive tackles worked hard to protect their quarterback, but the Aces linemen paved the way for Hammer again and again. Even when he hit Bill illegally and his team received a fifteen-yard penalty, he was not deterred. Fans were booing the Aces, who had not scored in the game and whose only aim seemed to be to badly hurt the popular Buck Mason.

In the third quarter, Bill went down hard and lay on the field for a few moments. Janice winced when Billy called him a sissy and told him to get up. As though he heard his son's taunt over the miles that separated them, Bill got up without help, and the fans cheered wildly. The score was 28-0 in spite of the Aces' defense. Bill was angry now and was clearly determined to increase the lead even more.

Scott Lansing talked to Bill on the field and motioned to the coach to have the second-string quarterback warm up. "Save it for the Broncos game," Scott told Bill. "Let Joey take over. We've already got this game won."

Bill waved him away in irritation, shaking his head. He was not about to quit. Nobody—and especially not Jared Hammer—was going to chase him out of a game. His son would never respect a quitter. Besides, Bill told himself, he still had a trick or two up his sleeve. In the huddle he gave the men the word that it was time for one of their specialty plays.

The puzzled Mavericks took their positions on the Aces' forty yard line, wondering why Buck was using a play usually saved for pulling out a victory in the closing moments of a tight game. It was fourth down with one yard to go—why weren't they punting? Bill glanced at Hammer briefly, and the man gave him a wicked grin.

Bill called the signal—"355, 421, hut, hut, *hut!*" Center Mark Potter snapped the ball to Bill, who quickly handed it to running back Keith Peal. It looked like a simple sweep as Bill dropped back, and Peal headed toward the left end. But suddenly he stopped and flipped the ball back to Bill, standing alone on the Aces' forty-five yard line waiting to pass to Scott, who was free and clear in the end zone.

Hammer, not fooled by the "flea-flicker" play, stayed in his position and headed toward Bill for the sack. This time he would finish him off before he could pass.

Bill saw Hammer coming at him out of the corner of his eye, but his powerful arm did not fail him. The ball was gone, and Scott reached up to catch it.

Hammer had worked hard for a long time to perfect his sacking technique. His specialty was downing the quarterback after the ball left his hand, yet making it look as though he merely had not been able to pull back in time. In his drive to disable Bill, he lowered his head and drove all of his 260 pounds into Bill's rib cage. Bill went down with a resounding thud, and Hammer landed squarely on top of him. At the same time, Hammer's helmet hooked Bill's helmet, which flew off as Bill's head snapped back. An intolerable pain ripped through the quarterback's body, and then everything went frighteningly black.

The fans cheered wildly at the touchdown play. Then their attention went to the fifty yard line where Buck Mason had been knocked senseless by the powerful linebacker. Bill's teammates were gathered around him, and the television announcer began to comment on the drama being played out before them. The scene of Hammer hitting Bill was replayed in slow motion from three separate angles.

Janice trembled as she watched the television, feeling as though she herself was the injured one. Frankie and Alice held hands tightly, watching Janice and the television at the same time.

The camera zoomed in and showed Bill lying motionless on the field. Blood covered his face and seemed to be coming out of his mouth.

Billy watched closely. Even *he* had felt the pain by the third instant replay.

"Get up," he said to the television screen. "Get up, you sissy. Come on, get up. Can't you take it?"

An ambulance appeared on the sidelines, and concerned paramedics bent over Bill. The announcer predicted grim news as the paramedics checked for signs of a broken neck or back before lifting the fallen athlete onto the stretcher. Hammer had done this to other players as well; all who witnessed what had happened hoped it would be the last time.

Billy pounded the bed again, and his voice grew louder. "Get up, you bum! Get up and walk off. Get up! Get up! Don't let him do that to you. Dad, get up!" he screamed.

"Billy!" Janice sobbed as she rushed to his hospital bed and put her arms around the trembling boy. Frankie came over and gripped the boy's hand.

"Okay, you guys, we gotta pray now. We gotta pray real hard, okay?" Struggling with his own emotions, he said, "Please, God, make Buck be okay. Make him be okay! Billy needs him, Father. I never asked anything like I'm asking now. Lord, don't let Buck Mason die!"

The rest of the game played before their unseeing eyes as they waited for some word about Bill. A feeling of desolation filled Janice when she realized she did not even know whom to call.

Scott Lansing rode in the ambulance with his friend, then nervously paced outside the emergency room. Doctors, nurses, and other personnel hurried back and forth, but none of them had time to answer Scott's anxious questions.

He found a phone and called his wife to bring him a change of clothes, then asked the uniformed woman at the nurses' desk to keep reporters away. He could not trust himself to talk to them right now. The woman called for hospital security officers, who stood watch to keep the persistent reporters outside that wing of the hospital.

Scott tried to sit down, then stood to pace the hall again. He saw a tall, middle-aged woman striding toward the emergency room and recognized Dr. Joyce Bennett, sister of team owner Ryan Brooks and a diehard Mavericks fan.

The emergency room doctor came out at that moment, and the two doctors conferred.

"He has an acute abdomen and is in respiratory distress. We started intravenous fluids immediately using ringers lactate and also gave him oxygen," the eager young doctor said, looking for Dr. Bennett's approval.

"Good," the woman answered. "I'll get ready for surgery. Bring him up right away." She turned and marched down the hall.

"Dr. Joyce!" Scott called after her. "Wait!"

"Not now, Scott," she shouted over her shoulder as she disappeared into the elevator.

At that moment the emergency room door burst open. The young doctor guided the side of the fast-moving gurney carrying Bill's unconscious form, an aide pushed from the far end, and a nurse walked briskly beside the gurney, holding up an IV bottle attached to Bill's arm.

Wincing as he looked again at his friend's battered face, Scott matched their pace.

"You've got to tell me what's happening, doc," he said. "Please."

"We're taking him to surgery right away. He has extensive internal injuries. It looks . . . Listen, if you know how to pray, I suggest you do it," the doctor urged. His face told the whole story. This was Buck Mason! They had to save him!

"Another thing," the doctor added. "He kept saying 'Janice.' Does that mean anything?"

"Yeah, it does," Scott said. He glanced once more at Bill as the elevator door closed between them. He went toward the telephone again, but the fear and anger raging inside him were too much. He sat down in a chair beside the reception desk, his head in his hands.

Lord, Lord . . . don't let him die. God, I'll kill Jared Hammer if Buck dies. O God, don't let him die! Scott pounded his hands together as he prayed. After a moment he regained at least some measure of control of his emotions. He knew he wouldn't be any help if he gave in to his anger.

The game was over, but the five spectators in the small trailer in Colorado sat numbly watching the post-game confusion. The reporters were hounding Coach Speer for news about Buck Mason, but as yet he knew nothing. There was speculation on the part of the sports commentators that perhaps the Mavericks had lost their chance to defeat the Broncos in the AFC championship game now that Mason was out for the season. There were guesses about the extent of the quarterback's injuries and talk about other players Hammer had injured. Frankie finally turned off the television in disgust.

"Listen, they don't know nothin'! It's gonna be all right, you hear?" he said firmly. Inside he prayed, *God, please make it all right.*

Billy stared at the television, shaking his head. Wasn't this what he had wanted? Didn't he tell Buck he wanted to see him get hurt? Then why didn't it feel good? Why was he going crazy thinking about Buck's unconscious form lying on the playing field?

The sudden sharp sound of the telephone startled them all. Janice answered, and an unfamiliar voice spoke.

"Janice, this is Scott Lansing, a friend of Buck's."

"Oh!" she cried. "How is he? What's going on?"

"I have to be honest with you, Janice. It doesn't look good. I know you're a Christian, so keep praying for him. We don't want to . . ." His voice broke, but he cleared his throat and continued speaking. "We don't want to lose him. I know things aren't all patched up between you two, but I think if you would come out here, it would help him."

"Yes . . . yes, I want to come. I'll try to catch a plane right away," Janice answered. She would use the money Bill had been sending for Billy.

But Scott quickly added, "I think I can get you out here faster than a commercial flight can. One of our team owners lives in Colorado Springs and has a private jet."

"The man Bill flew with when he came here?"

"Right. I'll call him. I know he can help. Then I'll call you right back," Scott said.

"Thank you, Scott. Thanks so much."

The others listened attentively. Alice said, "I'll get you packed. And we'll take care of Billy, so don't worry about anything, okay?"

"No," Billy said. "I have to go, too."

Janice stared at him. "But your leg, Billy . . . It's only been a couple of weeks since your surgery. You can't even walk on it yet. You might undo the healing that's already taken place."

"Mom, I don't care," he pleaded. "I don't care about my leg. I have to go!"

"I'll carry him to the car and to the plane, Jan," Frankie offered. "I think he's right. He ought to go."

Janice looked from one to the other, then nodded. "We'll have to pack your pain pills. Let's hurry."

Their emotions were placed on hold in the rush of preparing to leave. Scott phoned again, saying Ryan Brooks, part-owner of the Mavericks, was on his way to the airport and would be in Pueblo within forty-five minutes.

"Put this on," Alice ordered, shoving the pink mohair sweater at Janice, who stood numbly in the bedroom. Alice then ran to her trailer, found a suitcase, and put together other necessities for both travelers. Soon Frankie was driving them to the airport in an old station wagon Mac had bought him.

They were met there by Ryan Brooks, an exuberant man in his fifties who had begun planning his flight to Los Angeles the moment his star quarterback was injured. He gladly took Janice and Billy along, hoping their presence would ensure his star player's recovery. He, his steward, and his copilot made their two guests comfortable in the luxurious private jet.

It was not until the plane started down the runway that Janice remembered that neither she nor Billy had ever been in an airplane, and she was suddenly terrified. She immediately turned to her new source of strength and prayed, *O Lord, I'm so scared. Take us safely to Bill, please. Please let him be all right. Please let me tell him that I love him.*

Her hands clutched the arms of the plush chair, and she felt her heart in her throat as the plane rapidly gained altitude. They would have to clear a 12,000-foot mountain pass soon after take-off, and it seemed to Janice that they were going straight up.

"Lord, help me. Lord, help me," she whispered over and over. She took slow, deep breaths to dispel the nausea that threatened her.

The plane leveled at 20,000 feet, and Janice loosened her seat belt, venturing a look at the San Luis Valley far below. The sun, which had just set at takeoff, was visible again. They would gain an hour on the trip west.

The steward came into the cabin and offered Janice and Billy some refreshments. Both declined. Janice was afraid to eat anything because of the air travel, and Billy felt too heartsick.

The worried boy looked out the window at the mountains that carpeted the earth, but his eyes saw none of it. In his mind he kept replaying the scene of Hammer slamming into his father for the last time, the helmet flying off, and then the blood on Buck's face as he lay unconscious on the field.

I did it to him, he thought. *I wished he would get hurt, and he got hurt. But I don't want him to die. No matter what I said before, I don't want him to die!* He laid his head back against the head-rest and closed his eyes, causing tears to roll down his cheeks.

"Billy?" Janice said. She touched his hand. "Does your leg hurt? Do you need a pain pill?"

He shook his head. His pills would not remove *this* pain.

They were silent for a while. Then Billy said, "I don't want you to work at the diner anymore."

"What?"

"Promise me," he said.

"Why, Billy? What on earth . . . ?"

"I . . . I don't want you to work so hard. Frankie's there now. He can help Mac." He struggled for the right words. "I don't like the way those guys look at you."

"You mean the customers?"

He nodded.

"Why does that bother you?" Janice inquired.

"I don't know. It's just that you're my mom, and I don't like the way I see them look at you."

She thought for a minute. "Is it any different from you admiring a girl at school?"

"I don't look at girls," he answered.

"You do too, honey. I've seen you," she said. "Besides, people look at people all the time. It's part of life. It doesn't make me bad. I just ignore those guys. Being a waitress is good, honest work. I have to support us somehow."

Billy turned to stare out the window again. She made it sound so simple: work hard, ignore creeps, ignore the lies people told about her. She was a good person. What other people thought didn't make her bad. Billy tried to understand, but he was too tired to sort out his confusion.

As Janice considered their brief exchange of words, she began to understand Billy's unyielding bitterness toward Bill. He had always been protective of her, even as a small child. Now she could see that her son was angry because his father had not been there to protect her from the looks of other men. Maybe in time she could help him to believe she had brought some of it on herself when she ran away after the divorce.

Lord, I know You are doing something in each of our lives, she prayed. *I want to trust You with Billy's problems and with Bill's life. Help me know that You really do work everything out for the best, just like the Bible says.*

As she prayed, peace flooded her heart, and she relaxed for the first time since the game had started that afternoon. She was sure her feeling of peace was a promise from God that Bill would be all right.

SEVENTEEN

The stabbing pain and the feeling like he was drowning were gone. Bill felt himself floating on a cloud as blackness faded and a soft glow appeared. He looked through a mist and saw Janice and Billy far ahead. They glared at him as he reached toward them; then they slowly turned and drifted away. Now before him was a football field. The Super Bowl! But a large, raging bull appeared and raced toward him. It was Jared Hammer! Alarm filled Bill as the bull drove him away from the stadium while all his teammates shook their fists angrily at him. *No, no, I'm sorry! I've lost it all. I've lost everything!*

The scene vanished into smoke, and again the pleasant blue glow filled his vision. A bright pinpoint of light appeared and began to grow. Bill felt safety and indescribable peace surrounding him. There was someone there. Warmth! Happiness! It was the Lord! How good to finally see Him! Bill felt himself rising, reaching toward the light. *Jesus, Lord, I'm ready. Let me come live with You.*

"Buck Mason, don't you dare die, do you hear me?" a woman's stern voice shouted. Suddenly the light vanished. There was a flash of pain, then blackness again.

Dr. Bennett worked skillfully to treat the damage to Buck's lung where the broken ribs had pierced it. After draining the blood from his lungs with a chest tube, she made an incision to open his abdomen and then removed his ruptured spleen. Her hands were steady as she concentrated on her work, but another part of her mind worried. Why wasn't Buck fighting? Why was he just letting go? This was not like him.

"Let's keep him with us, people," she encouraged her surgical team. "Four units of blood," she told a nurse who quickly went to prepare it. Dr. Bennett glanced at the anesthetist, who gave her a nod. Buck's heart rate had evened out again. If he started slipping away again, they would bring him back, whatever it took. She was not going to lose him!

The trip took far less time than Janice thought possible. The plane landed at a private field near Los Angeles. Ryan Brooks and his steward helped Billy into the large limousine awaiting them, and soon they were on the freeway, far exceeding the speed limit in their race to the hospital.

Reporters and fans thronged the main entrance of the private hospital, although Janice was too concerned about Billy's discomfort to notice. She was only aware that the limousine drove around to the emergency entrance where a man she recognized as Scott Lansing waited with a wheelchair for Billy. With few words and much haste, the men guided Janice to a back elevator that delivered them to a fourth-floor waiting room. They joined several of Bill's teammates, and also Coach Chuck Speer, and another man, shorter than the rest, who introduced himself as Dr. Miller, Bill's pastor.

Janice had faded in and out of reality during the trip on the plane and in the limousine. Now that she was here at the hospital, only a short distance away from where Bill lay, reality stared at her harshly. Pastor Miller took her aside and told her that Bill's surgery was over and he was in the recovery room, but his condition was guarded. The doctor was still with him.

As the pastor briefly described the injuries to Janice, she felt fear rising in her heart again. The peace she had experienced on the plane slipped away as she began to focus on the possibility that Bill could die at any moment. The irony of it all made her desperately sad. Three months ago she might have found a grim satisfaction in his death. Now she wanted him to live more than she wanted anything else on earth. She wiped tears from her cheeks as the pastor talked of the doctor's concern at Bill's seeming lack of will to live.

If only I had told him I love him, she thought. *Oh, Bill, please live—for me, for Billy.*

After the flurry of welcoming the newcomers, silence came once more to the waiting room. Occasionally one of the men would bow his head in prayer, in anguish at the thought of losing not only a teammate but a good friend. Janice sat next to Billy, letting him lean his head against her as he sat in the wheelchair, his left leg propped up by a sturdy brace. His face was pale, and he was listless, but no one tried to cheer him or his mother. The whole world seemed suspended in an awful, fearsome pause.

The sound of the elevator door sliding open caused the group to look down the hallway. Groans escaped a few of the men as Jared Hammer stepped off, flanked by two of his fellow Aces.

Scott clenched his fists and slowly rose from his chair, but Jeff Pearson and Mark Potter held him back as he attempted to bolt toward the intruder. Scott jerked away from his friends, then turned and walked in the opposite direction. Never in his Christian life had he felt such hatred. He wondered how he could be expected to forgive Hammer if Buck died.

The three men advanced slowly as though they expected trouble. Jared looked defensive, defiant, proud. Then his eyes fell on Janice's slender form and the boy in the wheelchair. He looked down and wiped his brow. "O God, what have I done?" he whispered. When he lifted his face to them, there was genuine guilt and sorrow written on it.

Janice had been watching him come toward the waiting area, and it began to dawn on her that this was the man who was responsible for Bill's condition. Her eyes asked an anguished "Why?" as she stared up at him.

That look cut him to the heart. It was one thing to hit a man in athletic competition—to even hit him hard enough to put him out of the game permanently. That was his job, he had always boasted. But when he saw these defenseless people who also had been wounded by his action, it was too much to bear. He had never looked beyond his own bitterness toward Buck Mason to see who else might suffer, but now . . .

The great bear of a man looked down and said, "Ma'am, I'm real sorry for . . . for what happened today. I'm really sorry."

Janice looked away, unable to speak.

Then Jared knelt down by Billy. As cruel as he could be in a football game, he still cared for children. When the boy turned and looked at him, he stared. It was like looking into Buck Mason's face!

"Kid, I didn't mean to kill your daddy." His voice broke as he spoke.

Billy looked at the man. "Yes, you did," was his toneless reply. Then, burying his face in his mother's shoulder, he whispered, "And so did I." But only Janice heard his last words, and she held him closer.

"I can't handle it, man," Jared said to his friends. He rose and stumbled toward the elevator, his shoulders slumped forward.

Dr. Miller followed the three men in hopes of sharing God's love with them. His own heart burned with resentment over the senselessness of Bill's injuries. And yet he knew God's redemption was for everyone, even the Jared Hammers of this world.

Dr. Joyce Bennett gazed with motherly concern at the pale, scratched face of her patient. How she loved her boys! She had been treating injuries for the Mavericks for fifteen years, but this was the worst one yet. Buck was such a good young man, such a rascal, but one she would have been proud to call her own son. At times like this she wondered why she liked football so much.

All the players were like overgrown adolescents. All except evil gorillas like Jared Hammer.

She had adopted her brother's team as her own family. Despite her status as a well-known and respected surgeon, she baked cookies for them every week during the football season and never missed a home game.

She had raced from the stadium to the hospital just moments behind the ambulance when Bill had been injured. Now she sat at his bedside, having done all she could in surgery, watching his vital signs closely in case he coded again. The scratches on his face were superficial and must have occurred when his helmet had been knocked off. He had a mild concussion. One side of his jaw was swollen, but no teeth were loose. He would make it, she told herself. *O God, let him make it!*

She sighed deeply, then stood and checked the IV the nurse was adjusting, and wrote medication instructions on the chart on the end of the bed.

"Let's talk to him, Miss Holt," she said to the nurse. They both leaned over the bed to try to awaken him. "Buck, come on now, wake up. The world is waiting for you. Can't let the fans down. Come on, Buck, honey. It's Dr. Joyce. Let me see that gorgeous smile of yours."

Bill moaned. Why couldn't they just let him go? Why couldn't he just rest?

"You've got some visitors, Buck. Forty-four Mavericks running all over this hospital waiting for you to wake up! Talk to me, honey."

His eyes began to open against his will. Who was that? Janice? No, it was good old Dr. Joyce. He smiled, or at least made an attempt.

"Good for you, Buck. Come on now . . . All the way. Nurse Holt here wants your autograph."

"Hi," he mumbled. "Who won the game?"

"Well, the rest of the team won, but I'm not too sure about you."

"Hey, I got 'em twenty-eight points. Whaduya want?" he mumbled.

Dr. Bennett laughed with relief. He was okay. He even remembered the score. He was going to make it!

"Look, honey, we've got to clear out that waiting room. You about ready for a visitor or two?" she asked.

"Mmmmm," was his affirmative reply.

At the sound of the door swishing open, the waiting-room visitors turned to see the tall, gray-haired woman march through. The victory smile that lit her face broadcast the good news before she spoke. "He's going to be fine!"

"Praise God!" Scott and Jeff exclaimed in unison with Pastor Miller. The other men slapped each other on the back, and Chuck Speer pounded the coffee table, spilling the untouched beverages there. Janice and Billy cried happily, hugging each other as much as they could with Billy's chair in the way.

"Well, come on," Dr. Bennett said, "who's going to welcome him back?" Her eyes searched the room and rested on Janice.

"I can't yet," she answered through her tears. "I'm shaking too much."

"I guess I'm elected," Scott said and accompanied the doctor to the recovery room.

"Give him some encouragement, Scott," the doctor said. "He has a long way to go."

"I have a feeling he's going to get plenty of encouragement from the two people who count the most, doc," Scott said.

As he entered the room, he paused a moment to get a grip on his emotions and to adjust to the IV in Bill's arm and the nasogastric tube on his face. With a deep breath, he advanced to the bedside.

Bill looked up through a haze and smiled as he recognized his friend. "Hey, buddy, did you get the number of that truck?" he mumbled weakly, his words slurring together.

Scott swallowed the rising lump in his throat as he gently gripped Bill's hand. "Man, I've never been so close to killing somebody in my life."

"All I could think of as he came for me was how I wished I hadn't put off witnessing to him." Bill laughed softly, then winced in pain. The anesthesia was wearing off.

"Listen, there's someone here who wants to see you," Scott said.

Janice slipped quietly into the room and studied the man she loved. She had never seen him sick or injured. The swelling of his jaw and the scratches looked terribly out of place on his perfect face. Seeing the tubes and needles, she grimaced. Dr. Bennett stood nearby.

"Janice," Bill murmured, "how did you get here?" He tried to wake up.

"Hi," she whispered as tears began to escape from her eyes again.

"You wore my heart," he said. "That's the heart I gave you, isn't it?"

"I haven't taken it off since Christmas."

He tried to sit up, to extend his hand to her. Why was he so weak? He laid back and closed his eyes. "I'm sorry."

She took his hand and touched it to her lips. "I brought someone with me."

He opened his eyes again. "Billy?"

She nodded.

Once again Bill tried to pull himself up, but the pain was too much.

Dr. Bennett gently pushed his shoulders back. "I think he'd better rest now," she told Janice.

"Please, doc. It's my son . . . I have to see him," Bill said.

The winsome look in his boyish blue eyes made the doctor

wonder again how he could have a twelve-year-old son. He was just a boy himself!

"Will you promise me you'll stay calm and not try to get up?" she said.

"Mmmm," he said with a nod.

Janice left the room and moments later, with Scott's help, pushed Billy's wheelchair through the door.

Billy looked anxiously at the form on the bed and struggled to keep from crying as he viewed his father's battered face. The tube in Bill's nose made the boy feel sick to his stomach. But he impatiently forced his chair closer to the bed and pulled himself up on the side rail.

"Billy, your leg . . ." Bill protested.

"I have to tell you something," the boy said urgently, struggling to balance on his right leg despite the rising pain in his left one. "It's my fault you were hurt. I wanted you hurt real bad," he said quickly, knowing he could not stand the pain much longer.

Bill blinked back tears that blurred his vision. "No, son . . ."

"I wanted you hurt, but not like this. I'm sorry about . . . about everything." He gripped the rail of the bed fiercely. "Please just tell me why you waited so long to come find us." He put his head down. "No, no . . . I didn't mean to ask you that."

Bill's head suddenly cleared, and a chill swept through him. "Billy, I don't know . . . I wish I knew. Please forgive me. Please?"

Billy nodded, gritting his teeth as he reached to take his father's hand in the Mavericks victory grip. "It doesn't matter. I love you. I really love you, Dad!"

Bill returned his son's grip as well as he could and stared into the boy's eyes. "I love you, too, Billy. We're going to make a great team, son."

Billy nodded again. Then he allowed Janice and Scott to help him sit back in the wheelchair. He didn't want his father to see how much this had hurt his leg.

As Scott wheeled the boy from the room, Janice came again to the bedside. Glancing across at Dr. Bennett, her eyes requested a few more minutes with Bill. The doctor returned a smile. She would allow it, but she would watch him closely.

Bill lay quietly resting, his eyes closed as he savored the precious moment of reconciliation with his son. Then he remembered Janice and sighed with relief when he found her still there. She was so beautiful!

Janice returned his gaze, her eyes tender with love and glistening with tears. She had to tell him now. No more waiting. She reached out to take his hand again.

"I love you, Bill," she whispered.

He looked at her uncertainly. "You're just saying that to make me feel better."

"I am not." She laughed softly. "I really love you."

He tried to think of something smooth and clever, but all he could get out was, "Honest?"

"Honest!" She giggled again, sniffing back her happy tears.

He closed his eyes again. Was this real? He sure hoped he wasn't hallucinating.

"You want to get married, Janice?"

"Do you think I'm going to let anyone else nurse you back to health?"

"Oh, no," he groaned. "This isn't how I planned it."

"I know," she said. "You really like to be in charge, don't you? You wanted to do everything for me. But this way I get to take care of you. I need that. I need to be needed."

He smiled sleepily. "Well, I sure do need you, my beautiful Janice. Oh, yes, I need you."